Clarissa and the Wallflower

ARDOR POINT

LEYA LAYNE

For those who hide in the shadows and those who hide in the spotlight. I see you.

Chapter One

CLARISSA

I pull my Acura MDX up to the flower shop, and a smile spreads across my face. Getting out of the SUV, I lean on the hood and watch the activity that has taken over the huge parking lot. It's finally lumbersnack season! Tall trees, hot men, and holiday cheer are just what I need to be my obviously perky self. I smooth down my black lace miniskirt that barely covers my ample ass, make sure the ribbons laced up the backs of my fishnet stockings are straight, and then check my hair and makeup in the rearview mirror of my car before making my way inside. I know the moment all eyes turn toward me because the commotion stops. The aesthetic was originally meant to piss off my bougie ass mother, but it has its perks otherwise. I wave at old Nick when he turns his white-bearded face my way and then step inside the shop. Time to get a rise out of Carol.

Carol Platzchen is my boss and by all counts my best friend. She gave me a job here in the flower shop during my junior year of high school and has been a solid rock in my muddy ass life ever since. Truth be told, she's more like the big sister I never had but always needed, and like all little sisters, my greatest joy in life is to rile her up.

"Have you seen all the Christmas candy outside?"

Her eyeroll is perfection. She's absolutely perfected it over the past decade.

"I've not seen them, but I've sure as hell heard them!"

I grab the flowers I'll need for my first couple of arrangements from the coolers and make my way back to the counter where she's working. "You sure you haven't peeked?" I raise my eyebrows suggestively, putting the bunches on the counter.

"You're incorrigible," she says with a scowl that doesn't match the sparkle in her eyes.

"And you love me! Besides, there's nothing wrong with a little prick every now and again." I hold up one of the roses, to emphasize the double entendre.

She turns back to the casket spray she'd been working on, and her lip quivers. She always gets so emotional whenever we lose any of the older townsfolk. Though she hadn't grown up in Ardor Point, our little mountain hideaway has grown on her.

"Do you want me to do that for you?" I ask, putting my hand on her shoulder. For someone who claims to have sworn off men and love, she's the most sentimental person I know. Her reluctance to give up this particular task is a testament to her affinity for the old man who used to come into the shop religiously to get his wife flowers. "You know that tears on the petals won't make them last longer, right? I bet you could find one of those lumbersnacks out there to last longer, though," I tease, gyrating my hips in her direction. I burst out laughing at the half snort, half groan she gives me.

"You need some damn help!"

"That's what my therapist tells me too," I say with a wink and go to help whoever just came through the door.

Santa Claus stands there in the entry, at least that's what we affectionately call Nick the Christmas Tree Guy because his name, profession, white beard, and hearty laugh all scream Santa. I even offered to sit on his lap and tell him what I wanted for Christmas the first year he brought the pop-up shop to Carol's parking lot, much to her chagrin. I break out into a wide smile for the old man.

My smile falters as I take in the collection of men standing behind him. They're much younger than in previous years, closer to my age. A couple of them are ganglier than the typical tree guys Nick brings with him, though they still look to have some strength to them. Two are tall and the others are shorter, yet they're still taller than me if I take my platform boots off. I quickly take these men in, sizing them up, without lingering on any of their faces. Their gawking is enough to put my smile back in place until I'm skipping up to give Nick a hug.

"Santa! What kind of presents did you bring me?"

As if possible, the mouths that were gaped open, drop even lower. I step back, giving Nick a wink. He knows, or at least believes, I'm a harmless flirt. Who am I to change his image of me?

"Carol is in the back grabbing a few things. We're always glad when tree season comes around. It's nice to have big, strong hands available during the holidays."

Nick chokes back a laugh, and I giggle. The look on Carol's face when she comes down the aisle nearly makes me double over with laughter. She, rightfully so, is not so sure of my 'harmless' nature. These guys look like they'd be willing to take a chance if I let them. I mean, Carol doesn't affectionately call me the Pied Piper of Ardor Point for nothing. At that thought, and Carol's admonishment that Mrs. Jenson would be here any moment for the bouquet I've yet to finish, I furrow my brows and walk back toward the counter. Of course, I have to add a little extra sway to my hips as I do so.

Mrs. Jensen walks in almost immediately after Nick and his crew leave. Carol barely tolerates the woman, but she makes me laugh. She's been trying to get a read on me since I was a teenager. The old town historian, as she likes to call herself because 'gossip monger' sounds harsh, has sworn multiple times that she's seen me places I've never been with people I've never met. It's like she feels the need to make up stuff if she can't find out anything true. So, of course, I have to throw hints at false exploits as often as possible just to see who she shares her information with. If she only knew what I really do when I'm not here working, she'd clutch her damn pearls and probably choke herself with them. Who knows, though, maybe that would give her the little thrill that's been missing from her life.

She's in rare form today, though. Carol must've pissed her off on her way in.

"Good morning, Mrs. Jensen. I'm wrapping up your flowers right now," I say with my biggest smile and bright tone that contrasts starkly with my black and pink outfit and thick black eyeliner and lipstick.

"Hurry up, girl. I have far too much to do than to wait for something I have on weekly order."

My smile only grows at her condescension. I've been talked down to my whole life. Hell, my mother could give her lessons.

"Yes, well…"

Before I can get my snarky comment out, Carol walks toward us with a raised brow, basically telling me to shut my mouth. She comes behind the counter, grabs the beautifully wrapped bouquet, and hands it over to that old mean-spirited…

"Snake," I say a little louder than intended. At Carol's smirk, I whisper, "I should put a snake in her next bouquet. It would be fitting." I can see Carol's eyes roll in profile as she watches for the shop door to close behind Mrs. Jensen.

As soon as the door chimes, I pounce. "Who's the hottie with the beard?" I'm naturally attracted to older men. They seem to be better able to handle me and my interests.

The look in Carol's eyes, though, makes me think twice about pursuing that guy. She tells me he is too old for me, but then she agrees that he's hot. I'm sure her ass is attracted to him, I mean, who wouldn't be, but she won't admit it for the sake of her man-ban. Poor woman has been dry since she got here. It'd be good for her to wet her whistle, but she won't listen to me. Maybe Mr. Hot Ax will talk her into climbing his tree.

We spend the next couple of hours working side-by-side, as she finishes the flowers for Mr. Moore's funeral. I'm really just watching to make sure she doesn't break down like she did while working on the casket spray. Those are always the hardest for her and the ones she insists on handling personally. When the bell chimes again that someone has entered the shop, she walks toward the workroom wiping tears from her eyes.

"I'm on it," I call out, rolling my eyes at her back while the swinging doors squeak on their hinges. It frustrates me that she won't let me help with the preparations that bother her most.

Before I can round the corner of the aisle, I come face-to-face with Mr. Hot Ax, and my breath catches. He's even better looking than I could tell from the back of the shop. Shit, no wonder Carol was taken with him.

"Clarissa, right?" Even his voice is sexy as hell.

He's obviously a city slicker, but he has a bit of a slow drawl that warms me from the inside out. *Carol likes him*, I remind myself, and flash him my cordial, customer-service smile rather than my let's-play-rodeo smile and nod.

"You're Santa's grandson, right?" He turns to look out the window like he's confused by my statement. "Old Nick? White beard? Christmas trees?" Finally getting my reference, he laughs, but it's hollow. Something's amiss. "How can I help you?" I ask to break the tension.

He finally works through whatever is on his mind and holds out his hand. "Jackson Branch. I was wondering if you would be willing to share the best lunch spot in town. My guys and I need to get something to eat."

My eyes brighten. It wasn't exactly an invitation, but far be it for me to turn away from an open door. "Absolutely! Let me tell Carol I'll be back, and I'll show you the best place around." He thanks me and leaves to gather his guys. I can barely contain my excitement as I walk back to the workroom. Standing in the doorway, I try to hide my grin. "Hey, do you want me to bring you anything back from lunch?" Carol raises a brow, but I ignore it, smirk, and head back out the way I came.

Chapter Two

CLARISSA

We don't have a ton of options in Ardor Point because it's a small town in the Appalachian foothills, but Casey's Diner is the best place to go for lunch. Thankfully, Jackson came to ask early enough that we might just beat the lunch crowd. Especially since there will be six of us, we need to get there early to get a table. Though Jackson easily looks the part of the lumberjack tree farmer with his henley shirt and five o'clock shadow, the group of guys working for him don't match anything like what Nick had been sending us for the past five years. Usually, it's a group of tall men with heavily muscled upper bodies who looked like they could pull a tree from out of the ground, roots and all. This group seems like he picked them up on the side of the street.

There's a tall, lanky blond named Freddy. He has a few scars on his face, probably from early teenage breakouts. Puberty was a bitch for all of us. Though he seems to be cutting it up with the other guys, like they quickly built a rapport since Nick threw them together, there's something hard and cold in his eyes. He makes me a bit uncomfortable when he looks my way.

One of the other guys is Travis. He hasn't stopped staring at me since he walked into the floral shop earlier. It's almost like he'd never seen a woman before, or maybe he'd never seen one who openly expresses herself before. He seems pretty uptight and closed off. I immediately wonder what he would do if someone called him a little bitch and told him to get on his knees. Likely come in his pants is my guess.

Peter seems quieter than the rest, like he would sit back and watch but rarely participate. He stands out, though, with his bright blond hair and piercing blue eyes. Maybe he isn't so much quiet as solidly aware that people, women especially, will be drawn to him. He'll be a true daddy when he grows up, and I nearly fan myself at the thought. Normally, I lean away from the Nordic look because of my mother and her family, but I might be convinced if those eyes land on me at the right moment.

Finally, there's Marc. He doesn't say much, but what he has contributed to the conversation is meaningful. The thing is, though, if he wasn't interacting as much with Jackson, I might forget he was here. It's not that he isn't relatively attractive either; it's more that he has a baby face to go with his shorter and stockier body. He reminds me of the football players from my high school. I do like listening to him talk though. He has a nice low drawl

"Thanks for showing us around, Clarissa," Jackson says with a smile as we wait for our food.

"No worries. I love our little town...at least most days. I'm surprised Nick didn't give y'all the rundown."

Jackson seems to shrivel into himself. Though he has a half smile plastered on his face, I've learned to read body language. It's a safety mechanism. When you grow up with a narcissist, you learn many things to protect yourself. Jackson is not happy about whatever happened with Nick today.

"Nick didn't tell us shit," Freddy says, his voice matter of fact, as if he's fully participating in the conversation. His eyes, however, linger on our waitress, Mandy, and a shudder runs up my spine. I quickly cross him off any and all lists of potentials. His stare makes me uncomfortable, which makes me feel bad for the girl receiving it. Still, his words are surprising.

"All of you are new, right? I don't remember seeing any of you in the previous seasons."

Travis nods solemnly, and Peter shares that they'd all just met less than a week ago.

"What do you mean you just met?"

I can feel Jackson's anger simmering below the surface, but he holds that smile. He's obviously pissed about the situation but trying to play it off. I'm not sure if the facade is for my benefit or that of the young guys with him.

"Nick hired me a week ago today," Marc says as a simple explanation. He must have read my confused expression because he continues with his story. "He came into my hometown and sat outside the grocery store with a sign that said hiring. I was looking for an excuse to skip out on working the family restaurant this winter, so I took him up on his offer."

"Everyone else has a similar story," Jackson adds, his voice duller than it had been earlier when we were all chitchatting about nothing. "Well, everyone except me since Nick is my grandfather. I came to town a little more than a week ago, and he told me I would be the foreman for this shop."

My mouth drops open, but before I can say anything, Mandy brings our food. The table grows quiet as we all dive into our meals. Most of the guys are eating burgers, grease glazing their lips and running down chins, and I have to admit that Casey's has some of the best burgers ever. I bite into my cheesesteak with extra cheese, thankful none of the guys look at me crazy for my food choices.

When we get back to the shops, after I show them where the hotel and nearest grocery story are located, I can't wait to run inside and tell Carol about the situation Nick created. There is no way that shit was unintentional or fair. This is his business, and it's like he just said 'fuck it' for this year. I would've never imagined it from the old man, though I get the feeling Jackson has an inkling of why Nick just abandoned them all like this. Carol is as dumbfounded as me. Of course, I can't just leave her to ruminate on that negative situation. Nope, I have to change the subject to something far more interesting.

"So, I got three and a possible with that group of young guys." She stares at me mouth wide open. I don't know if she'll get the reference or not, but I'm not going to clarify. Instead, I push the envelope a little further. "I agree with you that Jackson is most definitely a hottie, but he's too old or at least too serious and boring for me." I don't add that he only turned serious when the conversation changed to Nick's behavior or that Jackson is obviously still upset about it. Per my job as little sister, I leave her staring after me with her mouth gaping like a fish. It's glorious.

Chapter Three

CLARISSA

Though we haven't started our seasonal hours yet, I'm already tired walking into the shop. I will need every drop of this huge coffee I'd grabbed on the way in. I can't have Carol asking too many questions about my nighttime exploits. Usually, I balance my after-hours work with my daytime job, but last night's session went a little longer than expected. Not to mention the fact that it was an intense weeknight session. I really try to keep those to a minimum, but it's hard to turn down a client willing to pay double.

"Girl, you look like you had a busy night," Carol says after taking one look at me.

I freeze, unsure what to say. The noise from the tree tents breaks through, and I manage a quick, "I don't remember them ever starting this early." I gesture with my thumb toward the windows looking out onto the parking lot. I don't bother to remind her that they've already been here a couple days now. I'm trying to take the attention off me, not make her even more suspicious.

"Don't change the subject. You never stay quiet about

your nighttime activities. So, which of the three and a possible was it?"

I let out a relieved breath. She thinks I'd spent time with one of the new guys outside. I silently thank whichever of the gods sent them here early in the season. "That possible was a little too easy," I say, putting a little smugness into my voice. Carol shakes her head, and I can't help but notice that she, too, looks a little off this morning. Since she's never bothered with men before, I don't bother to ask why she looks so tired.

The morning continues in the same pattern of weirdness. First, Carol's car won't start, so she can't make the deliveries. Of course, she won't let me do them because of the funeral flowers that she simply has to hand-deliver herself. While I hate the feeling that she just doesn't trust me, I know it's more likely her need for emotional catharsis. Then, in a surprising turn of events, she allows Jackson to be her chauffeur for the day. I would've never expected that.

I also didn't expect Freddy to come sauntering into the flower shop right before lunch asking if I'd like to join him. If it had been any of the other guys, and if I hadn't been here alone, I might have taken him up on the offer. I just can't get over how cold and distant his eyes are, or the fact that he already made me uncomfortable during our group lunch on their first day here. Nope, not taking that chance. In fact, I keep watching the door, hoping someone will come in because I don't want to be alone with him here either.

"Sorry, I can't leave the shop unattended, and Carol would kill me if I closed for lunch rather than wait for her to return."

"It's cool," he says, though there's something in his voice saying he isn't happy with my response. "Maybe next time."

"Maybe," I reply, keeping my voice upbeat. Thankfully, I know how to school my emotions and maintain a positive demeanor through all kinds of uncomfortable situations. Still, sweat beads along my spine as I look past him toward the windows. "Is Marc waiting to go to lunch too?" I ask as soon as the baby-faced kid comes into view, his face turned toward the shop.

Freddy turns away, surprise entering his voice when he, too, catches sight of Marc standing outside looking this way. "I don't think so." Without another word, he shoves his hands into his pocket and leaves the shop.

I place my hands on the counter to center myself. Freddy didn't do or say anything to trigger this flight or fight response pulsing through my body, but I still can't brush off the unnerved feeling he's left behind. I watch him go outside and speak to Marc before walking off toward the street. Marc's eyes never leave the shop door, and for the second time today, I let out a breath that had been caught in my throat.

An hour later, the sound of sirens fills the air, and cops swarm the parking lot. Now, this is a small town, so by swarm, I mean every cop on duty is here, a whole three cars and two unmarked SUVs. The first two exit their vehicles and approach the tents. Marc meets them outside, and I watch the emotions that play across his face at whatever they tell him. His expression goes from surprise to confusion to incredulity to anger to worry.

The other guys come out to surround him, and I find myself walking toward the door. His eyes catch mine right before I push it open, before the bell can chime, and he slightly shakes his head. I'm not usually one to follow directions, especially not from a man, but there is something in his demeanor that says I really don't want to be out there. As soon as the cops leave, Marc walks toward the flower shop, his emotions schooled and his steps steady.

Chapter Four

MARC

I don't know why I feel compelled to be the one to tell Clarissa what's going on, or why I had silently begged her to stay inside the shop while the cops were here. It's not like we know each other well. Shit, I barely know these dudes I work with. Considering what the cops just told us, had I known, I would've gone into that flower shop earlier and dragged Freddy's ass out of there. As it was, I had been uncomfortable the whole time he was in the shop alone with her. It sucks that my feelings were justified.

Clarissa seems like a girl who can take care of herself, but she's flirtatious as hell. Flirting with the wrong person can, unfortunately, cause trouble, and that damn Freddy is trouble. I'm still seething at the story the cops just told me as I walk toward the shop. If it wasn't for the woman behind the door whose gaze I feel watching my every step across the parking lot, I'd be out looking for Freddy my damn self, fear of confrontation be damned. Yet, she's there waiting, and she's been watching.

Her charisma and ability to catch the attention of everyone with her style of dress and big personality are magnetic, but she's more than that. She's enigmatic and everything I'm not. I knew I had no chance with her from the first day we all went to lunch. I saw how she looked at Jackson compared to how she looked at the rest of us. Clarissa has a thing for older men. Still, I want to be near her, to be in her presence, to soak up the energy she exudes.

She opens the door as soon as my foot hits the stoop. There are worry lines etched across her forehead, and I have the urge to reach up and smooth them out. She's far too beautiful to let worry mar her face. Without warning, she grabs my hand and nearly yanks me through the open shop door, quickly closing it and turning the lock.

"What in the hell is happening?" she asks, concern and curiosity vying for prominence in her voice.

"What was Freddy doing in here earlier?"

Clarissa's expression changes immediately. Her eyes narrow. "Why does that matter, Marc? You could've come over here if you had wanted to know." Her voice holds nothing of the friendliness or flirtation I've grown accustomed to hearing this week. I feel myself curling in, the worry for her fizzling in light of her coldness. I hate confrontation, and this definitely isn't the type of attention I want from Clarissa. She must recognize the shift in my emotions because her eyes soften, and she begins to apologize. "Sorry," she says. "I..."

"You don't owe me an apology," I say. "You asked me a question, and I responded with one of my own. That was rude. Relevant but rude."

She scrutinizes my face for several long seconds before she nods and takes a deep breath. "I'm far too used to everyone questioning everything I do and every damn conversation I have. I'm sure there will be questions about why I'm talking to you in here and why the door is locked."

It's my turn to eye her skeptically. This isn't a young girl. Though she dresses provocatively, she carries herself with strength and self-assurance. "I wasn't questioning you. Not really." It takes a few minutes before she assures me that she believes my words. Then I tell her about Freddy and the diner.

"Wait, so he left here, went to the diner and tried to attack Mandy? Damn, is she alright?" I nod in response and go to say more, but Clarissa's facade cracks. "Holy shit! He had asked me to go to lunch with him," she says, her voice distant. "What if I had gone?"

"Don't get started with the 'what ifs,' Clarissa. You made the decision to stay here for one reason or another. Be glad you did. I am."

I don't know what makes me add that last part, but when she looks up at me, and her chin quivers slightly, I'm glad I said it. If anyone were to ask me anything about larger-than-life Clarissa, I'd have said she's made of steel. Until this moment, I never expected to see anything different than her head held high and her air of confidence. I don't know why, but I know she wouldn't want anyone else to see her this way, full of uncertainty. I gently take her elbow and lead her away from the windows toward the back of the shop. Seeing that there are two stools behind the counter, I make her sit down on one of them. As soon as her bottom touches the wooden seat, she seems to collapse.

"Hey. You're fine. Just breathe." I put my hand on her shoulder, and she leans toward me. I hold my breath for a second trying to figure out what to do. I keep to myself and try to stay as far away from emotional outbursts as much as possible. If Carol were here...Hell, if anyone else were here, I'd be hightailing it out the door and back to the tents as quickly as I could extricate myself from her arms. Her arms that slide around my waist as smoothly as my arm snakes around her shoulder.

I'd simply wanted to comfort her, but now here I am holding her. Holding her and being held by her, her chest pressed against my abdomen, her head on my chest. Not only do the emotions make me uncomfortable, but my body's response to her also has my breaths coming at uneven intervals. The words of assurance I had given her just moments before are now ones I need to heed myself. *Hey. You're fine. Just breathe.*

"What am I going to tell Carol? She'll never leave me alone in the shop again if she finds out I nearly went to lunch alone with him."

"Did you?" She looks up at me, tears pooling in her eyes, though she's not spilled a single one. "Did you nearly go to lunch with him?" I ask, trying to keep my voice soft.

At first, she doesn't say anything, just looks down at my chest again, and I feel a tightness grow in the spot where her gaze lingers. I don't want to think about what might've happened had she gone with him, and I hope like hell she hadn't even considered it. Finally, she shakes her head, her arms squeezing a little tighter around my waist. That simple gesture helps me relax enough to put my arms fully around her shoulders, pressing on her back until she has to turn her face to keep from being suffocated.

Chapter Five

CLARISSA

I can't remember the last time I'd just been held for comfort. Touched? Yes, for their comfort. Hugged? Yes, for their benefit. Held? For my comfort? Maybe when I was a little kid. Maybe before... Nope, not going there. It's time to get it together and fix my face.

Instead of releasing him, though, my arms tighten around his waist, and I bury my nose in his shirt. It's still morning, but they work hard over there, wrapping and picking up trees, yet he still smells so good. Like citrus and pine. There's a brightness and natural warmth to his scent, to his arms holding me close. I relax my arms, and he completely lets me go. A shiver runs up my spine from the sudden cold that creeps in. It isn't cold in the shop. We always keep it a comfortable temperature for the flowers, but the sudden loss of his heat plunges my body into the arctic. Who knew that was possible?

"Th...Thanks, Marc. I don't know what just... I never break down like that."

He looks at me from where he now sits on the stool across the aisle like he couldn't wait to get as far away as possible.

"You don't have to explain anything. That was a lot to process. Do you think you're ready to call Carol?"

"Oh shit, Carol! Have you told Jackson?"

Though his olive skin almost hides it, pink tinges his cheeks before he can look away. He shakes his head slightly. "I came here to talk to you first."

I give him a tight smile before stepping into the workroom to call Carol. I hate having to make this call, but thankfully, she doesn't ask for much information over the phone. I walk back out into the shop and am not surprised to find that Marc isn't here anymore. In his place stands the rest of the town. I'm more bothered by the fact that I didn't hear the door chime when he left. There isn't time to dwell on that emotion, however, because the shop is now filled with nosy neighbors who are doing much more gossiping than they are shopping. Carol can't get here soon enough.

It's less than ten minutes before Jackson's truck pulls into the parking lot. We are a small town after all. Without a word to the customer I've been helping, I run out the door to Jackson's truck as soon as shuts it off.

"You are not going to believe what happened," I say, almost pulling her out of the truck and toward the shop at the same time Travis accosts Jackson with the news when he opens his door.

As soon as she walks through the door, before I can explain anything, Carol lets her eyes sweep around the place, landing on each person's face who watches the windows. Quickly, she begins her polite greetings, making sure to call each person by name and asking if they need help choosing a bouquet or plant. Just as quickly, the shop empties. Carol is masterful at working a room, a real natural, and she can read the bullshit from a mile away. How she hasn't seen through me all these years, I have no idea.

Once she's rid the place of all the gawkers and gossipers,

we're left with two actual customers. When we get their orders ready, and they take their leave, Carol locks the front door and turns to me.

"Now, tell me what in the hell happened here."

I tell her about Freddy going off to lunch by himself, strategically leaving off the fact that he had asked me to join him initially. I want her to know what happened and why the cops were here, but not how I might've gotten mixed up in it all. I have to remind her which of the guys was Freddy and reassure her that Mandy hadn't been hurt.

"The cops told Marc that she was just shaken up a bit." Thankfully, Mandy had been carrying pepper spray in her pocket and was quick enough to use it before he could do any real damage.

"Did they catch him?" Carol asks as she takes a seat on the stool I had vacated not thirty minutes earlier. When I shake my head no, she deflates. "What could we have done to prevent this, Rissa?"

"Nothing. There's absolutely nothing you could have done to prevent it. The guy had issues, and I'm so glad I wasn't feeling his vibe." She nods emphatically in agreement. "Besides, if anyone should take the blame for Freddy, it's Nick. He hired everyone without so much as a background check. Now the guys are worried about Jackson once Nick finds out what's happened."

"What do you mean?"

I explain everything I've learned about how the team was put together thanks to my lunch dates with them. Nick had driven through neighboring towns finding random young dudes with no tree knowledge or experience and offering them jobs. Within a week, they were at the farm learning the types of trees and loading the trucks to come this way with Jackson, their foreman for the season. It's an absolute clusterfuck, and this is just one of the consequences. Anger rises in her eyes, and she reaches for the phone, probably to cuss out Nick, when someone knocks on the door.

"Please tell whoever's at the door that we're closed for the rest of the day."

I eye her skeptically. We've never closed early before, not since I started working here almost a decade ago. "I'm on it," I say without my usual enthusiasm. Every couple steps, I turn back to look at her and find her watching me through the mirror system we installed a couple years back to ensure we can always see any customers within the store from every angle. I recognize Jackson before I even get to the door to turn the lock.

"Hey Jackson. How can I help you?"

"Are you good? How's Carol? I'm assuming you told her what's going on."

He's talking so quickly, it takes a few extra seconds for my brain to process what he's saying.

"It was definitely a shock, but I'm okay. Carol took the news pretty well, I think. How are you?"

"I've been better. Can I talk to Carol? She'd already had a rough morning."

I smile at his concern. It's nice to know there's someone else looking out for Carol besides me. "Give me a second." I head back through the shop with a knowing smile on my face. "Jackson's here and wants to check on you. He seems to be worried." She holds her expression as stoically as possible, and my smile grows wider. "Something happened between you two while making deliveries." She shakes her head vigorously, as if that will change the truth.

"Nothing happened. I got upset while delivering the funeral arrangements, and he comforted me until I could stop crying. That's all."

"Yeah, yeah."

"Just let him in and give us a minute, okay."

Chapter Six

CLARISSA

My grin is so wide when I walk out of the shop that my cheeks start to hurt. I walk toward the tents and make my way inside. Normally, I don't give a shit about the trees or the men who work the pop-up shops, other than to ogle them. Holidays aren't a happy time for me. They're always too full of pretense and expectations. My mother uses them to show off and uses me as a pawn in her games of privilege. Thus, I try to stay out of the tents. Today, though, I walk inside with a purpose.

The set up is interesting with various aisles and signs showing the different types of trees and their prices. It's far more organized than I'd imagined. I wave at Peter and Travis on my way toward the back of the tent where the cash register is located. Marc is back there hunched over the small counter writing on a piece of paper. He doesn't register my presence until I'm within an arm's reach of the counter, and then he jumps back like I scared him.

"Sorry," I say with a small chuckle. I quickly sober at his serious expression. "I...I wanted...I" Shit, I can't get the words out. His head tilts to the side, though his expression doesn't change. I take a deep breath, letting it out audibly. "Carol and Jackson are talking, so I needed to get out of there. I wanted to come say thank you for earlier."

The seconds tick by at a snail's pace before he finally relaxes, and a small smile crosses his lips. I'm not sure whether his discomfort is because I caught him off guard or just because it's me.

"Sorry if I interrupted whatever you were doing. I'll leave you to it." I turn away, ready to head back to the shop. I won't try to force my presence on anyone who doesn't want it. I said what I'd come to say. Truth be told, I don't know what really brought me here in the first place.

"You're welcome," he says from behind me. "And you don't have to go."

I respond without turning, though I stop my feet from moving. "It's okay, really. I came barging in on you while you were working, and I realize you probably have more work to do."

"Clarissa, it's cool. I was just writing down inventory. Not that we sold much with everything going on today."

I nod in agreement and turn back around fully. He holds up the paper he'd been writing on as if to show me it isn't anything important.

"We're closing early today because we've not had much business either, or maybe because Carol needs time to process how she feels. Between you and me, I think she was about to tell Old Man Nick off when I mentioned how he'd created this team." Marc cringes, and guilt gnaws at me. "I didn't mean anything about you or the other guys. Like, I wasn't trying to say you all were like Freddy."

"I know you didn't mean anything by it, but you're not wrong. It's fucked up, and any of us could have been like that. Just so happens, Freddy was the one."

"I feel like I'm saying all the wrong things, so I'm gonna go. Again, thank you for..."

"Clarissa, you don't need to thank me. I didn't do anything special," he says, cutting off my words.

But he had done something special. He had done something for me that no one besides Carol has done in years—offered me comfort, and, well, safety. I felt safe there in his arms. Not only did he keep the panic away, but he gave me the space to process it all, even the uncomfortable parts. I've not felt safe to be vulnerable in years, especially not with a man. Their goal is always to see what they can get, and vulnerability becomes a liability quickly. I didn't get the feeling that Marc wanted anything. He'd seemed so uncomfortable, almost scared to touch me, and yet he held me because I'd needed it. I can't just let that go unacknowledged.

"If you all close early too, wanna hang out? I'm not in a rush to go home, but I also don't know that I feel like eating alone either." I hadn't meant to say any of the last part, but he looks so surprised at my offer that I'm afraid he's going to decline. I really don't want to go home early, and I'd be lying to myself if I say I want to be alone right now. The shadow of Freddy's invitation to lunch is still sitting on my chest. They haven't caught him yet, and I don't want to be out and run into him. "My treat," I add as an extra incentive, and his eyes narrow.

"You don't have to buy me dinner, Clarissa. You don't have to pay me to hang out with you." Heat flares in my cheeks. I scowl, and he smiles. This smile is much larger than any of the previous ones he's shown since I walked into the tent. "You've just been surprising me all over the place, and I..." He stops abruptly like he's about to tell me something and suddenly remembers it's a secret. "Yes, food sounds like a good plan."

"Okay," I say, my tone a little brighter than it's been since he first told me about Freddy.

I leave the tent and pass Jackson on my way back to the shop. I need to make sure Carol doesn't need anything before I leave for the day. We're just about finished with the closing procedures when Marc pokes his head in the door to ask if I'm leaving soon. I look at Carol, and she smiles.

"Don't do anything I wouldn't do," she warns in her best big sister tone. Carol is the closest thing to a sibling I will ever have. Of course, that means whatever she tells me to do, I will have to do the opposite.

"I plan to do everything you wouldn't do," I respond with a wink before grabbing my bag and heading out through the door.

Chapter Seven

MARC

My palms are sweating so much, I keep rubbing them on the legs of my jeans. Am I dreaming, or did Clarissa really ask me to hang out. Not in the way the whole team has adopted her as a lunch buddy since we opened the tree shop. No, she stood right there asking me to hang out, to have dinner with her. I'm still struggling to believe it after I'd made an ass out of myself earlier. The woman renders me speechless. She's so different from anyone I've ever met. Her personality is as effervescent as her goth-style attire is brash. Everything about her calls for attention. I've never been that guy.

I was the nerd in school, the kid who liked numbers. My parents pushed me to join the football team thinking that would make me more social, but I would have enjoyed working the concession stand more. And by working it, I mean cooking the food in the back and never talking to anyone. The spotlight was just never anywhere I wanted to be. Still, they'd pushed me to attend parties and dance at all the family events. Before I took this job, they'd insisted I worked at the family restaurant. I wouldn't have minded too much if

26

they didn't want me to stand right out front and play host. The number of times I asked to run the business end, manage the books, or just about anything that kept the old women, tipsy from their top shelf margaritas, away from me. That's why I jumped at the idea of working the tree shop. Not only was it something new, but it was out of town and away from the expectations of my family.

Today's events aside, this has been the best job I've had since I've been old enough to work. The team is small. There isn't much time for partying and mayhem, and Jackson has turned out to be a real good guy. He lets me manage the inventory and somehow notices when I need to step away from a customer, or even the team. After dealing with the cops and then Clarissa's breakdown, I needed the alone time. I hadn't been prepared to look up and find her standing there like my mind had conjured her or something. But there she was, her blond curls highlighted in the colors of the Christmas lights we have hanging from the tent poles, a stark contrast to the tattered black jeans and oversized black and hot pink sweater she wore. She caught my startled expression and got defensive. I could tell by the way she stumbled over her words. I just didn't know what to say to make it better. My brain froze with the realization she was there to talk to me.

Now, here I am standing outside the flower shop waiting for Clarissa like a puppy she'd tied to the stoop. When she comes bounding out of the shop door with the biggest smile on her face that I've seen all day, I want to ask about it, to know what suddenly has her feeling better. Instead, I wipe my hands off once again and put a smile on my own face, afraid to see hers fall.

"I was thinking," she says, her tone nearly back to its normal brightness. "Do you like to bowl?"

"Sure," I respond with a bit of a shrug. This woman has been catching me off guard all day. There was no way in hell I could've been prepared for that random question. Just when I think I've run through all the possible scenarios, she knocks me off kilter at every turn. Somehow, I don't hate the feeling.

"Good! After all we've been through today, we deserve good old-fashioned fried food. None of that fancy prime cut meat or healthy salads. We deserve beer and wings!"

I can't help it. Laughter bubbles out of me. Her mouth drops open in what I can only imagine is mock surprise because she immediately whines out a drawling, 'what?' Before she stomps her feet in indignation.

"Don't tell me you don't like wings."

The unexpected response only makes me laugh harder. This has to be a joke. "I love wings so much," I say. "I could eat you under the table."

She doesn't immediately respond, but her lips pucker together, and one eyebrow raises. "Interesting," she finally says, her smile returning, though some of the playfulness is gone. I rack my brain trying to figure out what just happened. She stands there watching me with anticipation as I play through my words. They were meant to be a fun little challenge, but...*oh shit!* Heat creeps up my neck into my ears and across my cheeks when I finally realize what I said.

"No, wait," I sputter. "I simply meant that I could eat more wings than you. It was a challenge, a joke." I'm tripping over myself, but I can't stop. We haven't even gotten into the car yet, and I'm already ruining it.

Suddenly, she bursts out laughing. "You're cute, and that is why I'm going to take you up on that challenge, and I'm going to win." A devilish grin takes over her face, and I'm once again rubbing my palms on my jeans. She takes my arm and leads me toward her SUV.

MARC

"Should we start off with ten wings? Ease you into it?" Clarissa asks with a smirk.

After her response to my unintended double entendre earlier, I have the urge to respond in kind, but I'm still not sure what this is. Are we now friends? Did she invite me because she thought she owed me for being nice to her earlier when she needed comfort? Will she think I'm flirting?

"Earth to Marc. Are you in there?"

I raise my eyes to hers, and the look on her face says that she's waiting for a response. Wait, had she asked me something else? "I'm sorry, what was the question?"

"How many wings should we start this competition off with?" There's no judgment or accusation in her tone, though there is a shift in her expression.

Ugh, why is this so hard? Why can't I just act like a normal guy? My runaway thoughts are, thankfully, interrupted again by a server who comes by to take our order. That is not a service I expected in this little ass town's 25-lane bowling alley. We sure as shit don't have that service in my hometown's alley.

"Let's start with twenty and up the ante."

Clarissa's head swivels around to me, and her smile makes my breath hitch. There's mischief in her beautiful expression. She doesn't say anything, though, until the server leaves to put in our order.

"First things first," she says, turning fully toward me, "where did you go earlier when I asked for the wing count?"

Heat blooms in my ears. What would she think if I say I go into my own head during uncomfortable situations? Would she laugh? Would she make fun of me like my family does? I'm used to their ridicule, but I don't want that from Clarissa. I want to be the straightforward, macho, don't-give-two-fucks dude around her, but that's just not me.

"I have a bad habit of overthinking things," I say with a self-deprecating laugh.

"And what were you overthinking about? How many wings you could eat?" I shake my head but don't respond. Finally, after several excruciatingly long seconds, she nods. "So, about this ante," she says while putting on her rented shoes, the red, white and blues ones typical in bowling alleys. Who knows how many pairs of feet have been inside of these bits of leather, and why am I even thinking about that when Clarissa is about to decide the prize for the person who eats the most wings? I say nothing until her pensive gaze locks back on me. "What are you willing to bet?"

"No ma'am, you first. I may have issued the challenge, but you accepted it without terms and then offered to 'ease me into it.'" This time I'm ready for her surprise, as I know exactly what I'm doing by throwing her words back at her.

"Well played, lumbernerd."

Time stops. Is she mocking me? Did she let me off the hook with her previous question just to make fun of me now? I feel myself spiraling again and quickly give a hearty chuckle before asking, "Lumber what?"

"There are lumberjacks," she says nonchalantly, "which is

really any guy who cuts down trees. Lumbersnacks are hot guys who look like they cut down trees. Sometimes they do, but they don't have to. You might be either of those two, and you're a lumbernerd. You're a man who works with trees and probably knows a shit ton about them because you pay attention to details and want to know more."

My heart is racing by the time she finishes. There's so much in that description, I don't even know where to start. "We weren't even talking about trees."

"That's the best part. We didn't have to be. You caught my little joke earlier, held onto it, and threw it back at me in a well-timed jab. I bet you know a hell of a lot more about trees than anyone else on your team."

"Knowing about them makes them easier to sell," I say defensively, and her eyes gleam.

The server brings our wings and beers. As soon as she walks away, Clarissa leans in. "Thank you for making my point."

Damn, she has a quick wit. I shouldn't enjoy being on the receiving end of it, but I am, in fact, enjoying it. I tip my head at her. She's won that small challenge, but I will win the big one. "You still haven't made your ante yet," I state before passing her a small tray with half the wings in it.

"Okay, fine. The loser pays."

"That's it?" I eye her skeptically. I haven't known Clarissa long or well, but she doesn't seem the type to bet so little on a personal challenge.

"And," she draws out before a long pause, "the winner decides on the next hangout."

The first bite of food hits my tongue, and the buffalo sauce slides down the back of my throat right as she finishes her statement. I gasp. Okay, I choke because she's implying we'll hang out again. I hadn't been expecting that any more than I'd been expecting her to be so genuinely playful with me. At our team lunches, she's cracked jokes, some sexual, but it hasn't been easy to tell how much of the personality is real and how much is her need for attention. Maybe, the attention-seeking is the facade because the wit is real. Just because I've been enjoying her company, though, doesn't mean she's been enjoying mine. I'm sometimes too reserved for others, too quiet, too shy, too pensive, too introverted.

"I'll take that bet and raise you the answer to two questions." Her eyes narrow as she studies my face. What could she possibly have to hide? Or better yet, what kind of questions does she think I might ask? I throw her a bone to keep the mood from shifting. "Here are the two questions: What's been your proudest moment and your biggest regret?"

Her head tips to the side, like she's contemplating my offer, and then she finally nods. Without a word, she lifts a wing in my direction as a sort of salute and pops it in her mouth. Seconds later, she pulls the completely clean bones back out. For the third time tonight, I nearly choke on my own spit. Not only am I going to lose this bet, but I'm going to lose it with an uncomfortably hard dick.

The next two hours pass by in a blur. We order two more plates of twenty wings, and she finally gives up when she's hit 25 total. Not gonna lie, I'd wanted to stop at twenty, but I pushed through to 26 total just to win at something today. I might not have pushed my stomach to that painful limit if she hadn't been kicking my ass at bowling too. I'm a decent bowler. It's one of the few sports I really enjoy because I don't have to deal with lots of people. Still, she's beat me every game. When she stands, ready to bowl her tenth frame of our fifth game, I realize my poor showing is because of her. I can't stop watching her, staring almost. Okay, I've actually been staring, and when I try to focus on getting my ball down the lane, she'll say something or laugh or just breathe, and I lose all concentration.

When the game is over, she grabs our shoes and struts up to the counter to return them and settle our tab. Her grin when she returns is infectious. "That was the best fifty dollars I've ever spent," she declares while putting on her chunky boots. "I seriously had the most fun, even if I did lose the bet."

"I did too," I say in agreement, my smile matching hers. This really has turned out to be the best day, all things considered.

"So, Mr. Wing-Eating Winner, what will our next outing be?"

"Does it have to be another competition?" I ask.

"Of course not, silly! You were the one who issued the challenge, not me."

"That's fair, though, in my defense..."

"No defense," she says, interrupting my argument.

"Fine, we're going to the movies. That's a safe space from challenges."

Her bright-eyed smirk tells me I might be wrong about that assumption. The wink she gives me before turning away tells me I don't really care.

Chapter Nine

CLARISSA

It was barely 2 o'clock when Marc and I got to the bowling alley. In my mind, we'd have a couple drinks, bowl a couple games, and just hang out, killing a couple hours before I needed to go to my other job. The other job that no one knows about. When it comes time to leave, though, I'm not ready.

Marc is a lot more fun than I'd expected. He's funny, even if he takes himself too seriously sometimes. He listens and genuinely cares about what I have to say, even when I'm talking nonsense just to try and get a rise out of him. I can tell that, like me, he just wants to be his own person. Still, I have obligations to keep, like paying customers.

Marc and I exchange numbers right before I drop him off at his hotel. We don't really have to give each other our numbers, since we basically work in the same place and see each other every day, but I want him to have it. I want him to know that I see him and want to be his friend. I throw my hand up in a quick wave as I pull away.

My job is an hour away, and then I need time to change and get ready on site. Though leather and lace are part of my everyday attire, my uniform is far more revealing than I can realistically leave the house in. Besides, the transition not only puts me in the right frame of mind but allows the anonymity I seek for the same reason I choose to work over an hour from home. No one can know.

I wave on my way through the staff door. "Hi, Cale. Busy Night?"

He grunts at me as I pass the long hallway to our prep rooms. Cale Rogers is a big, burly biker with a surly attitude. If his gruff exterior covered in intricately designed black ink doesn't warn off any potential trouble, his commanding voice has been known to stop men and women in their tracks. He's a case study of a man whose bark is as bad as his bite. Like now, my breath hitches when he grounds out, "One of your regulars has been here for thirty minutes."

"And he wouldn't see anyone else?" I ask.

It isn't unusual for subs to have their favorites, but I don't have long-term contracts with any of mine, which means they can see anyone who's available. I also don't have any regulars scheduled for tonight. I was told there were two newbie sessions.

Cale shrugs before adding, "He's not alone."

Now that is unusual. I've had sessions with couples before, but if the person waiting is a regular who usually comes alone, it's relatively unheard of, at least in my experience, for them to randomly bring a partner. I've also not met many men who'll come with their friends and be willing to admit they want to submit to a woman's dominance. Just like me, they want this place to be their secret, something they keep just for themselves.

"Thanks," I say, as I head to my room to change.

Because I only work here part time, I share a room with another Dom. We work opposite shifts or alternating days to allow each other privacy. The rooms are relatively spacious, giving us the opportunity to perform most of the acts our customers might want. If a session calls for special equipment, another room must be reserved ahead of time, but we never allow that for first timers. We need to get to know each other first, find out what their wants and needs are, and ensure we work well together before upgrading. Our individual rooms are big enough and equipped to handle couple sessions, though not groups. Those are exhausting anyway, so I don't participate in them often. This is a part time job for me to let off steam, not to burn me out.

I smooth my hands over the black patent-leather, Demi-cup corset that lifts my double Ds up perfectly while barely covering the dusty pink areolas. One day, these tits won't stand up like they do now, so I'm going to enjoy them while I can. My black panties hug my ass, outlining my thick thighs. I love the way they cup my fat pussy, holding my lips up enough that the material tickles my clit if I moved just right. I always make sure my clients get the pleasure they seek, but there is nothing saying I can't get mine too. I finish the look with thigh-high boots and a lace mask that covers the entire top half of my head and face.

Victor, one of my regulars, sits in a wing-back chair in the lobby. He's conventionally handsome with his short-cropped blonde hair and chiseled jaw. He has one leg crossed over the other, and that foot is wiggling back and forth like he's either nervous or impatient. If he's really been waiting without an appointment, it might be a bit of both. As my eyes travel over him from the shadowed hall, I finally notice his hand in the lap of the woman seated next to him. She's significantly smaller than him, petite in all ways. Her mousy brown hair is pulled up in a tight chignon and she looks out of place, like she's uncomfortable with the environment. Her eyes shift every which way whenever someone moves, and if they approach the couple, she flinches slightly, but she never releases his hand.

Double-checking myself in the mirror to ensure my face is covered, I put on my Mistress Ingrid persona and walk straight toward Victor. "Victor," I say in my generic Eastern European accent, pressing the leather flap of my riding crop against his chest, "you did not have an appointment."

He immediately sits up straight, pulling his hand from the woman's. "No Mistress. I'm sorry, Mistress." I can see the woman eyeing him suspiciously before looking up at me with something akin to awe in her twilight eyes. I want to smile and reassure the woman who appeared to be here against her better judgment, but I won't break character. Not only does Victor have expectations for my response, but anyone else watching in the sitting room will be waiting as well. The thing about these unscheduled sessions is that we are basically auditioning from the moment we step into the light of the room. Old clients, new clients, potential clients. They all have expectations. Breaking character, letting them see behind the mask, will ruin the experience for them.

"I was not prepared for your service today, Victor, so what have you come here to do for me?" I ask, still not acknowledging the woman at his side.

"My girlfriend insisted...wanted to come."

I tilt my head slightly before turning my eyes and running my gaze over her from head to toe. She turns the prettiest shade of pink under my scrutiny before defiance creeps into her expression. I had been thinking he was full of shit about her wanting to be here, but that slight change in her demeanor has me second guessing the thought. Maybe she did insist he bring her. She probably found his credit card statement or overheard him talking about me. That's the only explanation I can come up with for why he'd not only bring her but choose to wait so long when there are others working today.

"Did you want to come?" I address the double-meaning question to her, and her eyes drop to the floor, nerves and embarrassment emanating like waves. I place the keeper of my crop under her chin and lift her face, forcing her to look at me. "I asked you a question. I do not play with the unwilling, no matter what their partner says." Her nipples pucker beneath the sheath dress she's wearing. She isn't wearing a bra, and her body is telling on her way before she nods and gives me a weak 'yes.' I smile down at her and hold out my hand. "Come with me." She stands without argument or hesitation. When Victor goes to stand beside her, I lift my foot to his chest and push him back into the seat. "I will come back for you."

"What's your name?" I ask the woman. She seems to have shrunk since I pulled her to the back room. I have to get her to sign all the paperwork and need to double check without Victor present that this is something she wants to do. We have small reception rooms for initial consultations. They're little more than closets with two chairs, a lamp, and a small table. There are small doors on the wall that hold clipboards with contracts and confidentiality agreements. "Sit," I say when she still hasn't answered my question. "We will go no further than this room if you are unable or unwilling to talk to me. As I said earlier, I do not take anyone into my service who does not want to be here."

"My name is Cameron," she finally responds after a deep breath. "Victor and I are engaged. We've been living together for three months. I saw this random charge on the bank statement and asked him about it. He wouldn't tell me at first, but I insisted. I threatened to leave him." She's breathing rapidly and rambling at this point. "I thought he had another girlfriend, and I'm still not sure this doesn't count as cheating." She takes a breath and looks at me. "I forced him to bring me. I was hurt and angry that maybe I wasn't enough for him, but when he explained to me what you did here, I became more turned on than anything." Her cheeks turn crimson, and she averts her gaze from me. As before, I use the crop to turn her back. She takes another deep breath. "I wanted to see what you did for him that I don't."

"And do you still want all of that? If you come into my space, it is because you want to serve me, not to observe him. Do you want to serve me, obey me." She swallows audibly and nods. "Are you sure you can handle seeing your fiancée submit to me? Not everyone can, and that is okay." She again averts her eyes, and I lightly tap her leg with my crop, the slap echoing in the small, empty room. She gasps, but her nipples peak again, and she gives me a resolute nod. "You liked hearing him apologize to me, calling me Mistress, didn't you? I could see your nipples harden, just like they are now." She instinctively folds her arms across her chest, until I again tap her with the crop. "Answer me, Cameron, or I send you both home."

"Yes, I want to serve you and watch him submit. I want to learn to be more open with him." I smile and pull the clipboard from the wall, showing her the pages to sign. We settle on her safe word, which is different from Victor's, and we discuss what she is and isn't willing to try today. I hadn't planned for any couple sessions, but this one might be fun. I might even make her whip him, pushing both of them to their limits.

Once we finish the intake, I place her in my room, instructing her to strip and wait for my return with Victor. He and I negotiate payment before I bring him to the room, but once inside, he immediately steps into his role, stripping his clothes and kneeling at my feet.

"Why are you here, Victor?"

"For your pleasure, Mistress," he says without hesitation, leaning forward to kiss the toe of my boot.

Cameron gasps, and my body tingles in anticipation. Tonight will be fun.

Chapter Ten

CLARISSA

Normally, I would do two newbie sessions on the evenings I have no appointments, but Victor's surprise arrival with Cameron took the full time. I can't complain, though. I made more than those two newbie sessions combined would have been, but now I'm home and horny. The couple behaved perfectly, giving themselves over to me completely. Watching her come into her power when she took the handle of the flogger and brushed the falls over Victor's ass had me wanting to make him eat my pussy while she flogged him. I wasn't completely sure their relationship was ready to handle that level of intimacy with another person, so I squeezed my legs together and let my panties rub me into a dripping mess. It's extremely rare that I enter into any true form of physical intimacy with clients, preferring to focus on the mental and emotional intimacy that most of them look for. Tonight, however, left me wanting.

I reach for my phone, ready to find some kind of erotic story or video to help finish me off when I see multiple missed messages.

Marc: I had a great time. Thanks for driving me back to the hotel.

Marc: When did you want to go to the movies?

Marc: Did you make it home?

Marc: I hope I didn't scare you off.

I look at the time, shaking my head and feeling a little guilty. I mean, I couldn't have answered a few of his texts because I was working, but now it's so late, it would be awkward to answer. I flop back on my bed and continue scrolling my notifications. He called once about twenty minutes after his last text, probably to ask if I was okay. Then I see three missed calls from Carol more recently. I sit up instantly, bringing up my text thread with Carol.

Me: Hey, what's going on? You called me multiple times.

She doesn't immediately answer, and my heart rate picks up. Carol never calls or texts me once I've left the shop. If anything, it's always me texting or calling her, especially before I started my other job a couple years back. I used Carol as my safe space, the person I could release some steam on without judgment. Finally, the three dots blip across my screen.

Carol: Something happened at the shop.

Oh shit! I jump out of bed without sending a response and begin throwing my clothes back on. I type out a quick question as I pull my sweater over my head.

Me: Are you ok?

Carol: Jackson's in the hospital. Well, we're still in the emergency room. Can you come? Do you have a way to tell his guys?

Me: Oh shit! I'm on my way, and I'll let Marc know.

I slide my boots back on, grab my bag, and head toward the door.

"You just came home," my mother yells from her bedroom. "Where are you off to now? It's unbecoming for a woman to run around at all hours of the night. What will the neighbors..."

I pull the door shut before she can finish her question. I don't really give a fuck what the neighbors have to say. They already think what they want anyway. The only person I give a fuck about is Carol, and she needs me. As I put the key in the ignition, I press dial on Marc's number. I really hate calling him this late, especially after I ignored all his texts and calls earlier.

His groggy voice answers, "Hello?"

"I'm so sorry for calling you this late."

I hear him shuffling around, and his voice is much more awake when he responds this time. "Clarissa, are you alright?"

"I'm fine. I'm sorry I didn't get to answer any of your texts earlier. I wouldn't have called you back so late, but Carol just called me. Jackson's at the hospital."

"Do what now?"

"I can pick you up on my way, or you can meet me there. I don't have any other information."

"I'll be downstairs in the lobby in ten minutes."

Chapter Eleven

MARC

I send a group text to the others.

> Me: I just heard that Jackson's in the hospital. I don't have any details, but I'm on my way there now.

> Travis: Seriously? Do you need us to go with you?

> Peter: Yeah man, let us know what's up.

> Me: Clarissa's coming to pick me up. I'll let y'all know what's up when I get to the hospital. Keys are under the seat if you need the truck.

I'm closing the door of the truck when Clarissa pulls up, and I jump in the passenger seat. The first thing she does is yawn, and it's all I can do to stifle one right after hers.

"It's been one crazy day," she says, pulling out of the parking lot.

"You ain't kidding," I agree.

"Sorry to wake you like that. Bet you're regretting having given me your number." She laughs sardonically.

"Not at all. I just was…" I pause, unsure how to tell her what I was thinking when she never answered my messages. "I thought maybe you were tired of me after this afternoon. I'm not always the best company."

"Stop," she says, laying her hand on mine where it sits atop my knee. "I didn't lie when I said I had a great time. I just got busy after I left and by the time things settled down, it was already late. I feel bad about having missed all your calls and texts. I wasn't ignoring you."

I let out a deep breath. I really thought I'd come on too strong or was too much or too weird. All those things family and classmates have said to me over the years ran through my head, and I was sure Clarissa was thinking every single one of them too. "Okay," I say quietly.

"Okay," she responds. Still, she doesn't take her hand from mine, and I settle my attention on her warmth.

It's still relatively warm here for mid-November, but there's enough chill in the air that she has the heat blowing. Her hands are even warmer. I want to turn mine over and hold hers, but I'm afraid she'll pull away, so I stretch up my pinky and lock it around hers. The corner of her lip tilts upward, and I turn my head to look out the window before she sees me smile like a loon.

At the hospital, we find Carol sitting in the waiting room. Her hands are clasped together so tightly on her lap that her knuckles are white. Clarissa drops to the floor in front of her and wraps her arms around Carol's shoulders, pulling her close. I know they're tight, and they make a pretty good team in the flower shop, but I hadn't realized how deep their relationship goes until this moment. Carol's head is resting in the crux of Clarissa's shoulder, and she's sobbing. I take the opportunity to slip away to the desk and ask about Jackson.

The hospital doesn't want to tell me anything because I'm not next of kin or even related to him. I have to explain to multiple people that I'm his assistant at work and the closest one to him. I don't even have contact information for any of his family, except Nick, but without knowing what happened, I don't want to call Nick. Though none of us know exactly what's going on between the old man and Jackson, we know that Nick would use every misstep against his grandson. It doesn't make any sense, and because I like and respect Jackson, I won't do anything to make things worse for him by involving Nick unless I have to.

I walk back over to where Carol and Clarissa are sitting. Carol has stopped crying, though her eyes are a bit swollen, and Clarissa is sitting at her side, grasping her hand. "They said that Jackson has a concussion at least, and they want to do one more scan before they release him. It might be later tonight or early tomorrow. What happened?"

"Freddy was inside the tents when we got back from the bar," Carol says, her voice small. "He attacked Jackson, and they fought. Freddy caught Jackson off guard and landed a few good hits. Jackson couldn't keep his eyes open or even sit up by the time the ambulance got there."

"What happened to Freddy?" Clarissa asks, worry playing on her face. I hate that she's once again in a near panic because of that asshole. I can see it written all over her beautiful face, and I want to soothe the fear away.

"I don't know," Carol says, and Clarissa gasps.

"He's still out there?" she asks, looking around the waiting room like she expects to see him jump out of the shadows.

"No," Carol says, "I knocked him the fuck out with a shovel. Since I'm not in jail for killing him, I'm guessing he's either here in the hospital or in custody."

I watch Clarissa relax. Everything that's been tense is now loose, and a smile plays across her lips. I walk over and put a hand on her shoulder. When she looks up at me, I mouth a silent 'you good?' and she nods.

"I can take care of things here if y'all want to go home. There's no reason for all of us to be here."

Carol shakes her head. Before I can argue, Clarissa takes over, urging her to go get some rest.

"I didn't see your car in the parking lot or Jackson's truck. I'll take you home and then pick you up in the morning. I didn't bring any clothes with me, else I'd just stay at your house." Still, Carol continues shaking her head. "Carol, if we don't get any rest, neither one of us will be able to open the shop tomorrow. Jackson already won't be able to be there. You're the boss."

I want to argue that me and the guys can handle the trees, but I know the point she's trying to make. Carol looks dead on her feet. "Don't worry about Jackson. I'll make sure he gets back to the hotel whenever they release him, and the guys will keep the shop running. Now that you've taken out the concern of Freddy, things should run smoothly." I feel the need to cross my fingers at that last part, but I'm sure we can handle it.

Finally, she agrees to let Clarissa take her home. I use the time to go inside the ER and check on Jackson. He's asleep when I walk in. His head is wrapped up tight, like a mummy, and there are bandages on his arms and hands. Carol wasn't kidding about the fight he'd been in. I stand there watching the gentle rise and fall of his chest for a few minutes before he opens his eyes and focuses on me. His chin lifts.

"You good, boss man?"

"Yeah," he says, his voice hoarse. "Where's Carol? Freddy? What are you doing here?"

I smile at the barrage of questions. If he's able to remember all that enough to ask about it, he's going to be fine. "I just sent Carol home with Clarissa. She was falling asleep in the waiting room." Though there's a moment of sadness in his eyes, he nods. In an effort to make him feel better, I add, "The front desk wouldn't let anyone back here or give out any information. I had to argue with them that you had no close relations here other than our team and that I was your assistant. They were adamant about family only." He seems to accept that reasoning and relaxes back on the pillows rather than holding himself stiff.

"And Freddy?"

"Not sure. Carol said he's either here in the hospital or in custody because he was knocked out when the cops got there."

"Good. I wish I could get my hands back on him!" He starts to lift off the bed again like he wants to sit up, but his head sways.

"Boss, you're not getting anything or anyone right now. Just lay yourself back down."

He growls in frustration, and I chuckle. "I'm going to tell Clarissa to take me to the shop for your truck, and I'll have the other guys open in the morning. We'll make sure everything's taken care of. I'll be here whenever the doctors release you."

"You don't have to do that. You need sleep too."

"I'll sleep better knowing you're good. Now get some rest."

Chapter Twelve

CLARISSA

"Ugh, why do men act like fucking boys?" I rail as I walk into the flower shop. Carol comes out of the workroom with her head tilted and brow lifted in a question.

It has been days since the Freddy incident and things are relatively back to normal. Marc and I are spending more time together, hanging out and chatting long into the night. I still haven't told him about my other job, but he doesn't seem to mind when I don't answer him until after ten or eleven. I could call him on my hour-long drive home, but then he'll wonder where I'm coming from, so I usually wait until I get home and settle into my bed. Having someone to talk to who listens and doesn't judge has been nice.

Over the week, I've also learned so much about him that explains why he always seems so nervous. His family doesn't understand him, and they make him feel like he isn't enough, or that his wants and needs have no value. The first time he told me about being forced to work front of the house at his family's restaurant, I had tears running down my face. It's obvious he's an introvert, that he prefers to be in the background, and thrives in one-on-one spaces where he isn't the center of attention. The fact that his family can't see and accept that, can't accept him, breaks my heart. I know how it feels to have your family force you into situations that go against your nature. The selfishness and gaslighting hurt so fucking much. He's too sweet to deserve any of that. Not saying that I deserve it, because I don't, and I especially didn't as a child, but I've always been far more rebellious and assertive than Marc appears to be. I can take it.

Now, these fucking man boys he works with are ribbing him about spending all his time with me. He says he's fine, but I can tell it bothers him to get the unwanted attention. I want to tell them that Marc and I are just friends, but I know that won't make it any better. They either won't believe me, or they'll find some other reason to turn it around on him. I hate that for him. I want to protect him from their ridicule.

"So, how do you plan to get them back?" Carol asks me once I explain my anger and frustration. I simply stare at her. What could I possibly do or say to make this better for him? If I cause a scene on his behalf, it will just make him even more uncomfortable.

"I don't want him to regret the time we spend together," I say, my voice fuller of emotion than I want it to be.

"There is no way that man resents you. He was just in here a little while ago asking when you'd be back."

I can't help but smile. I know that my eyes often dart to the window of the shop hoping that the movement out there is him. We're friends, just friends, but I really like him, and I'd hate for his team to be the reason our friendship falls apart.

"Speaking of the team, I found out they don't have plans for Thanksgiving. They're going to be in the hotel."

"What do you mean?" Carol asks incredulously.

"I'm surprised Jackson didn't tell you that they weren't

going home for the holidays. What's going on between you two?

I don't really expect an answer. Carol doesn't talk about herself much, and I have no idea how she'd handled relationships or men before she moved here. In fact, Jackson is the first man I've ever seen her show any interest in for the past ten years. That's why I can't understand why she's so adamant that nothing is happening between the two of them. It's clear to everyone that their chemistry is running wild. Then, she tells me she feels the universe is conspiring against them. It makes me angry, and I'm ready to tell her to put on her big girl panties, but lucky for her a customer comes in before I can say anything more than, "Fuck the universe!"

Holidays with my family are miserable. Every year, I push through, just waiting for the moment I can escape to Carol's house. This year is even worse. She's preparing a Thanksgiving feast for Jackson and his team, and I'm stuck here unable to help.

"We're all waiting for Clarissa to start school again. She took some time off, but next semester will find her one step closer to medical school," my mother announces to her friends while I sit here rolling my eyes.

I do plan to go back to school, but I have no interest in being a doctor. Of course, being an artist isn't good enough for my mother. She will not accept anything that doesn't put her in higher standing. Even my stepfather, Henry, is nothing more than a boost for her ego. The man is ten years her junior and from a wealthy family. The fact that he is the fifth son and unlikely to inherit much doesn't mean anything. His last name still ties her to that family. Hell, half the people around the table are only here because she claims ties to the Danburys, Scotch moguls from Boston. I look at my watch, ignoring how Henry's eyes stay locked on me. As if this fucking dinner isn't uncomfortable enough, my mother's husband stares at me like he wants to have me for dinner.

When everyone finally retires from the dining room to whichever of the sitting, reading, or cavorting rooms mother has various activities set up in, I plan my escape. Henry stands at the top of the stairs, blocking me when I leave my room with my overnight bag.

"Where do you escape to all the time?" he asks. His eyes are piercing and his lips part as he looks me up and down.

Mother insisted I wear something less controversial, which really meant she wanted me in a colorful dinner dress. She wanted to show me off, and my dark clothes and matching makeup are inappropriate for the company she keeps. Like I give a fuck. Still, I must try and keep the peace until I'm ready to move out. The extra money I make at night is helping to get me closer to that moment. Right now, though, I just need to get out of the house.

"I'm going to Carol's," I say, trying to move around him to go down the stairs.

"Your boss? Why would you want to spend the remainder of the day with a florist?" He says the last word with a sneer. Rarely does Henry show his elitism, preferring to try and win me over with his smile and charm. Tonight, however, he's been drinking, and I can't wait to get away from him.

"She's also my friend, a real friend, not someone hanging around because she might get something from me." My tone is harsh, much harsher than I initially intend, but I'm already done with his haughtiness. I take that shit from my mother, but I refuse to deal with it from anyone else.

"I could be your friend," he croons, and bile rises in my throat. No fucking way.

"I have to go," I say, walking around him with my bag between us. If not for fear of tripping on the carpeted stairs, I'd run down them straight out the doors. Instead, I hold my head high and descend like the lady I'd been trained to be, though my heart is racing faster with each step.

Carol's dinner party goes off without a hitch. The food is plentiful and delicious. The company is much more enjoyable and the conversation genuine. The hours pass by with so much laughter my stomach aches. There are a few moments where I think Marc is going to lose his shit on the other guys for some ill-timed ribbing, but I'm able to calm him down. Though I want to see him break free of the reins he has on himself, this meal is so much better than the one I'd left earlier that I don't want anything to ruin it. I also don't want to ruin Jackson's plans for tonight. Carol deserves to have her socks rocked, and if making sure the team is still friendly when it's time for us to quietly leave the house unnoticed, that's what I'll do.

Any excitement I have upon leaving Jackson and Carol alone dies when we got to the hotel to find a woman, a woman who looks and sounds as phony as my mother, introduce herself as Jackson's fiancée from California. She claims that Nick gave her the hotel information, so she could come spend the holiday with Jackson. I immediately hate everything about her. I hate her thousand-dollar shoes and high ponytail. I hate that she's here and about to break Carol's heart. Most of all, though, I hate the gut feeling I have that she's somehow lying.

"I can't believe he had a fiancé and has been all over Carol damn near since we opened the tree shop," Marc says as soon as we jump in the truck to head back to Carol's.

"I can't believe she's telling the truth."

He looks over at me. "You think she's lying?"

"There's something phony about her. Jackson doesn't exude phony. I'm usually a pretty good judge of character."

"What gave you that idea from our short encounter with her?" I doubt he means to sound so disbelieving, but it irks the fuck out of me.

"She reminds me of my mother. Everything is for show. Nothing is real. She may know Jackson. They may have even had a thing back in California, but there is something about her that is not adding up with him planning to marry her."

"I hope you're right," he says, far quieter than he's been all evening. "I've always gotten good vibes from Jackson. If he's playing this kind of game, he's not a good guy."

"Agreed. I just hate that no matter what, tonight, Carol is going to get hurt while we work out what's true."

And I'm right. I watch her heart break when I explain who is at the hotel right after Jackson gives us both a sad look and leaves the house with Marc. He doesn't even bother explaining anything to her himself, which both surprises and disgusts me. Unfortunately, my anger at so many parts of the day bleeds out onto Carol when I accuse her of being just as phony as anyone else who might come to Ardor Point as a place to escape their reality. I'm tired of the pretense and the secrets, even though I, too, have secrets.

By the end of the night, I'm the only one left holding mine. Carol tells me everything. How her parents had all but abandoned her. How she had run away. How she'd entered into the world of kinks as a submissive, and how her ex nearly killed her with breath play. Her confessions answer so many questions about why we were able to grow so close so quickly, yet I still don't tell her about my sex work. She'd participated for release. I do it for power and control. Those are not the same things, and I don't want to diminish her experience by diving into mine. Instead, I bottle it all inside and fall asleep worn out and eyes puffy.

Chapter Thirteen

MARC

The past few weeks have been painful. We all walk on eggshells around Carol and Jackson. Between his guilt and her hurt feelings, we barely speak outside of talking to customers. When the parking lot is empty, the entire place is silent. More than once, Clarissa has come over to get away from Carol's moodiness, and there are days when I leave early to escape Jackson's pining at the tent opening. One day, Clarissa comes running over with tears streaming down her face yelling about how Carol and Jackson need to act like adults and actually fucking talk to each other. I see Jackson flinch at the accusation and quickly take Clarissa away from the shops.

Through it all, our friendship continues to grow. We tell each other everything, and we've even agreed to go to Christmas with each other's families to serve as a buffer. Everyone assumes we're a couple anyway, so we might as well take advantage of how well we've played the part. Not that I'm really playing. I've never felt so close to anyone before in my life. I'm falling for her. Scratch that, I fell a long time ago, but I won't do anything to mess up the good thing we have going. If she wants anything more from me, she doesn't show it, so I won't push for it. I will be nothing more than her friend if it keeps her close. It's bad enough that the end of the holiday season means we'll already be physically distant from each other. I'm not going to make the situation worse by making her uncomfortable.

That's why, when the other guys ask me to go out with them to this place they'd heard about in a larger town about an hour or so away, I agree. Jackson and Carol, after finally getting their shit together, go out of town, leaving us to close the shops for the season. Clarissa has plans for the night, and I don't feel like sitting around the hotel. Travis, Peter, and I will go out and celebrate the end of the season before we all go back to our respective hometowns. At least, that's what I thought was the plan until we arrive at this nondescript, warehouse-looking building with a dimly lit entry door.

"What in the hell are we doing here?" I ask.

"So, I was out the other day," Travis says, averting his gaze, "and someone approached me asking if I wanted to volunteer for a session with a dominatrix."

"Do what now?"

"A dominatrix. A woman who..." Peter starts explaining.

I don't let him finish his sentence. "I know what a fucking dominatrix does. What the fuck do you mean you volunteered? You volunteered the three of us to get our asses beat?"

"They don't do anything you don't want them to do, but yes. When the person offered me the spot, they said I had to bring friends." I give Travis a death stare. "Something about new trainees needing people to practice on while a more experienced hottie gives them tips."

I shake my head. I shouldn't be surprised that this is how these two morons would want to celebrate the end of the season. Nor should I be surprised Travis somehow wiggled his way into it for free. I let out a loud sigh and follow them to the door though I know I'm going to regret this.

We're escorted into a large waiting room with chairs set up around the perimeter. It's dimly lit with opulent trimmings, nothing like the outside of the building. I take a seat and level my glare on Travis. This is the last sort of thing I want to do. Not for the first time this evening, I wish Clarissa had been free. I'd much rather spend the evening with her doing nothing than be stared down by the huge dude standing near the dark hallway off to the side. He's gotta be some kind of security. I can't imagine anyone thinking of fucking around with that dude in the vicinity. Then I look back at Travis and realize there are absolute dipshits just roaming the streets.

Ever since Thanksgiving when Jackson's ex showed up out of nowhere, Travis has been babbling on and on about domineering women, women who exude strength and power. If I think about it too long, I start to believe he fucked that woman after Jackson kicked her out of his room. Hell, it would explain his behavior the next morning when she'd shown up and started shit with Carol. His ass was rooted to the ground right outside the tree tent watching, and he wouldn't move until she was gone. Yep, he's been obsessed with domineering women ever since.

The woman who checks us in says that our appointment is with a Mistress Ingrid and two trainees. I can't even imagine how someone trains for this kind of work. All I know is that I wish they'd come on and take us back to get this over with already. At least that's how I feel until she walks out from the dark hallway, passing by the security guy. She has on thigh-high boots with stiletto heels that have to be at least five inches tall. Her thickness makes my mouth water. Her thighs barely fit into the boots she's wearing, and the tops of those legs are wrapped tightly in what is either spandex or patent leather boy shorts. My eyes travel higher with each step she takes, and my mouth goes dry as I get to the point where her rounded breasts just about spill out of her black and electric blue corset.

I'm not one to ogle women. My parents taught me to be a gentleman but fuck if this woman isn't made for viewing. She has pouty lips painted a perfect red. The rest of her face is obscured by a lace mask that also covers the top of her head. Blond hair falls beneath the edges in the back, and I have the urge to run my fingers through it. No other woman besides Clarissa has ever taken my breath away like this. I can't stop staring, and when she speaks, I just about stop breathing altogether.

"Gentlemen," she says in an accent I can't quite place. Maybe Russian or Czech. Definitely somewhere in that region. "My name is Mistress Ingrid. I understand you've volunteered to serve me and my trainees for the evening." I look toward Peter and Travis. They're both nodding as if mesmerized, and I feel myself do the same. "I need your words. We do nothing here that isn't consensual. I do not play with unwilling partners." My two companions talk over each other to tell her yes. She turns her attention to me, but I have no words. If I answer honestly, I'll have to say that I don't want to be here, yet I sure as fuck don't want to leave now. "And you? Are you here to do my bidding?"

Something about that question directs all the blood in my body straight to my dick. I'm not a man who likes to fuck around. I'm not a virgin, but I'm selective. I'm also not sure what all will happen when she takes us to a room. It doesn't matter that she likely has multiple men on her daily roster. It's not like I plan to marry her, but something has me wanting to possess her.

She tilts her head and purses her lips. If I could see her eyes, they'd likely be narrowed as she waits for my response. She lifts the stick in her hand. It has a leather-covered handle with a loop at one end and a square piece of leather at the other end of the long shaft. Before she can do anything with it, I give her a solid 'yes.'

"Good. There is some paperwork you must fill out. While I normally do that in one of our small conference rooms, you are three large men who will not comfortably fit. Also, my girls need to get in the practice of conducting their consultations, so we will do so together in our group session room. Nothing will happen until the consultations are over." She looks at each of us, one after the other. "Are you ready, boys?" When we all say yes, she gestures for us to follow her down the long hall to a room at the very end.

Chapter Fourteen

CLARISSA

My heart races as I try to figure out some way of making it through this session. Bile sits in my throat since the moment I saw the volunteers for our training session. I had to run back to the room and warn Mandy to ensure she remains unrecognizable because we both know the men. After the situation with Freddy, Mandy was feeling helpless and scared. His attempted attack had really rattled her, and she was looking for a way to regain her power. I had no intention of telling her about the job, and I damn sure didn't plan to train her, but our conversation flowed in that direction, and she wanted to try. Though I'm loathe to admit it aloud, I still feel guilty about that day since he attacked her after I had rejected his invitation to lunch. I don't know the other girl I'm training. More importantly, though, I would like to know who the hell recruited our tree salesmen as fucking volunteers.

I feel three sets of eyes on my ass as I lead them to the group session room. Normally, that feeling would have me ready to perform. Now, it simply has me ready to run and hide. Fear holds me in a death grip. All I can think is that Marc will see right through my disguise. If it were just the other two, I could somehow encourage their silence, but his participation, his agreement to the session means I'll have to work with him. Marc is a sweetheart who doesn't want the spotlight. Though he seems intrigued, if not completely turned on, by my act in the lobby, I can't imagine him wanting to be denigrated publicly, even just in front of the other two guys who'll be getting the same treatment. If he responds well at all, it'll be to praise. He deserves praise.

A shudder runs through my body straight to my core at the thought. Marc and I have grown close these six weeks. I haven't allowed myself to think of him in any other capacity. Of course, he's cute, but my attraction to him has grown in relation to our friendship. The more I learn about him as a person, the more I like him. He's never seemed interested in me as anything more than a friend, so that is where I leave it. I stopped the flirting and sexual overtures. Instead, I focus on the things we like to do together and him as a person. Now that I have him here under my control, though, the lies I've been telling myself all seem to unravel. I want him, want him to want me. The heaviness of his breathing when I address him directly, and the way he looks me up and down, makes me want to pant along with him. Tonight is going to be a disaster.

Still, I take a deep breath and open the door, ushering the men inside. I'm nothing if not a professional. As soon as the door closes behind them, I look at each one directly before gesturing to my trainees. "In this room, you will address each of us as Mistress. Peter, this is Mistress Clara." I gesture toward Mandy. He is the least observant of the guys, so if she missteps, he'll be the one less likely to put the pieces together. "Travis, this is Mistress Edna." The trainee I don't know well steps forward, and he goes to stand near her, nearly vibrating in anticipation. He must have been the one to initiate this experience.

"As I told you all in the lobby, I am Mistress Ingrid, and I will be leading this session. Marc, you will help me demonstrate." I turn to him. "Do you understand the type of service you will be providing me today? If one of the other Mistresses asks to learn something, I will show them on you." Marc does not respond right away, and I see Travis swaying in my peripheral vision like he's itching to jump up and volunteer for my service. There's no chance that will happen. Finally, Marc answers with a quiet 'I understand,' and I let out a breath, thankful he hasn't changed his mind.

"Before we get started, there are forms you must fill out, and we will each conduct a short orientation to attain your level of consent and your current limits. It is not unusual to have inhibitions and discomfort with the unknown your first time. Please be as honest as possible with your mistress. We are not here to hurt you." Travis groans. I silently count to five. "We are not here to do any permanent harm. Hurt has varying levels from the pinch of a nipple clamp to the sting of a riding crop on the ass," I say, stepping over and landing a solid thwack on Travis' hip. He gives a little yelp, but his eyes blaze with desire. "Be honest with your mistress, and she will take care of you."

I had already walked the two women through the intake and orientation process before the men arrived, so they have their forms and list of questions to ask. We have our own designated area to sit and talk with each man. These areas are far enough away from each other that we'll only be overheard if someone intentionally raises their voice.

"On a scale of 1-10, how uncomfortable are you with being here?" I ask Marc, trying to gauge his enthusiasm. My Marc would not have initiated this excursion. He likely wants to bolt. Wait, since when do I call him 'My Marc?' Since when do I claim him? I slap my hand with my crop redirecting my thoughts, and Marc flinches.

"Can I be honest?" he quickly asks.

"Of course. I need you to be honest for this relationship to work." His brows lift at the word relationship. "Even if you choose never to come back after today, we are entering into a dominant, me," I say, pointing to myself, "and submissive, you, relationship." I point to him and then between the two of us. "Not all relationships are meant to last, and that's okay. You are welcome to be curious and uncertain at the same time. I do, however, need to know you are in this room and prepared to serve me of your own free will. You have the power to say no to any and everything."

I watch his face closely, and he lets out an unsteady breath. For some reason, his internal conflict makes me feel better. I don't want him to have come here tonight looking for this. Though I can see the effect I'm having on him by his heavy breathing and tented pants, I don't want him wanting Mistress Ingrid, the domineering woman with the clear agenda and straightforward, detailed plan. I want him to want Clarissa, the chaotic woman wearing the don't-fuck-with-me costume who uses sexual innuendo as a diversionary tactic.

"Mistress?" he asks quietly, pulling my attention back to the room. When my eyes focus on him again, he holds up the forms he's completed, and I take them from his hands with a nod. I stay silent because I don't trust my voice while I look over his responses to the important questions. His safe word is... I stifle a gasp.

The other day, he and I were talking about how other people see us compared to how we see ourselves. He told me that I stood out against the darkness like a poinsettia in the middle of winter. His fucking safe word is poinsettia. Jesus Christ I'm not going to make it through this night.

Shuffling on the other side of the room brings me back to the moment again. I have never been so distracted in this space before. Here, I'm on top, powerful and direct. I call the shots, and I can pretty much tell how things will go before I even give my first command. I'm far more distracted at the flower shop where I'm worried about making sure everything is perfect and beautiful. I get lost in the creativity of floral design. Now, one could argue that this work also requires a level of perfection and beauty, as well as creativity, but it's never the same for me. This man, though, has me off-kilter. He has me second-guessing what I'm even doing here, but the show must go on and all that. So, I stand, gather the papers from the other women, place them into the wall safe, and fix my face.

"Let's play, boys," I say, turning to face them all. "Strip."

Unsurprising, Travis is the first one to slip off his shirt, his shoes, his pants, and he is ready to drop his briefs. I tap his hand with my crop to stop him.

"For now, everything but your briefs. That is, of course, unless you aren't wearing any. Then you can bare it all."

Travis sulks, and I give his mistress a sideways glance. She smirks and slaps his thigh with her crop.

"Are you going to whine the whole session?" she asks him.

He purses his lips, brows furrowed. "I wasn't..."

She taps him again with the crop. "You weren't given permission to speak. You could've answered with a simple nod of your head."

I smile. She's going to do just fine. I can already tell that she likes having control. I turn my attention to Mandy who stands there watching the exchange like she doesn't have someone to tend to herself. My eyes glance over to Peter who is also watching Travis and his mistress. It's like the two of them are frozen in place, as if they are there to be spectators rather than active participants. Though I'm not surprised based on both of their personalities, I need for Mandy to be more assertive if she's going to successfully play this role.

"Mistress Clara," I say, gaining her attention. "Your toy does not seem to know how to follow directions."

Peter opens his mouth as if to say something, and she reaches over, closing his lips with her fingers pulling on them. "Do not speak," she says. "Strip." I nod my approval.

When I turn my head back to Marc, my breath catches. I had missed him stripping down to nothing. Literally nothing. There's a knot in my throat as I take in the beauty of him. He's an introvert, a wallflower, but he's built like a sculpture, hard and soft lines in all the right places, and he's packing. My mouth goes dry, and I want to drop to my knees. Instead, I reach out and cup his cheek. His eyes flinch slightly, wondering what I'm going to do after watching the other two women, but then he presses into my hand. "Good boy," I croon. "Continue to listen so well, and you'll be rewarded."

"Now, we are going to get each of you set up in different areas of the room, and we're going to play some games. If you like what we do, you will say 'Thank you, Mistress.' If you don't like what we do, you will apologize."

Travis, eager as ever, can't keep his mouth shut, and 'What?' flies out of his lips.

Just as quickly, his mistress grabs him by the hair. "I have just the thing for you," she says, pulling him backward toward the far corner. A smirk plays across my lips. He came to be dominated, but I don't think he really knew what he was asking for.

Chapter Fifteen

MARC

I like the way Mistress Ingrid looks over my body, appreciating every line. I may not be the star athlete my father wanted, but I take care of myself. I'm too short to not make sure my body is strong. Too short and too quiet, easy pickings for bullies. I refuse to make it any easier for them by also being physically weak. My physical strength gives me the fortitude to stand up for myself when I need to. That's another reason I like working for the tree farm. Lifting and wrapping trees all day keeps me in great shape. Even Peter who hadn't been very buff at the beginning of the season has started filling out in his arms and chest. I don't know what his plan is for after the season, but if he keeps up the strength training, he'll have all the women chasing after him.

There's only one woman I want chasing after me, or at least there was until this one walked into the light from a dark hallway. Now, all I can focus on is how much I want to continue being her good boy. I swallow hard when she walks over toward the wall of whips. Do I want to be whipped? I stand there staring at the wall for a few solid moments before I realize she's watching me. Her eyes travel up and down my body, and it takes all my concentration to keep from becoming painfully hard. From behind me, I hear grunts and groans. I can't tell if they're from arousal or pain. I need to tune them out, though, before I lose myself and wind up completely erect before her. Why in the hell hadn't I worn underwear today? Because I never wear underwear with jeans. Because I had no warning of what we were coming to do. Because it wouldn't make a difference if she keeps looking at me so intently. I can't see her full face, but I can see the play of emotions across her lips, and she appreciates what she sees.

"Tell me, Marc. Do you see something you like?"

Is that a trick question? I've been staring at her. I mean, previously, I'd been gawking at the wall of torture tools, but most recently, my gaze has been focused on her. And yes, I like what I see. Her head tilts, and I know she's waiting for a response. I want to make her happy, so I nod because I'm not sure what she'll do if I say what I'm really thinking.

"Use your words."

"Yes, I like what I see," I say, clearing my throat. She smiles, showing her teeth, and my heart stutters.

"You're going to be so good for me. You're going to listen so well. I can tell. Now, choose your fate." She gestures to the wall, though I'm sure she knows that I mean her.

Turning from her to the wall, I take in all the different instruments. Some I know the names of, like floggers and whips, while others are completely unknown. My imagination runs wild with the possibilities of how they might be used, and I swallow hard. Some handles look like dildos. Some of the straps look barbed. She said they'd do no permanent harm, but damn if many of those things don't look potentially painful. She stands with her body tilted away from the wall, so she can see me and the other guys with their mistresses. Something possesses me to move. Though I know she's there to train the others, I want all her attention on me. Her face turns to me, and her lips form a line. She isn't happy. She isn't smiling like she had a moment ago. I hate that I can't see her eyes. I can always tell so much about what a person is thinking from their eyes.

"Am I to assume your movement means you've made your choice?"

I nod. Before I can process what's happening, she taps my naked thigh with her riding crop. That's the name of it. I couldn't think of the name earlier, but as soon as it touches my skin, as soon as the sting processes, I know the word. *Fuck!*

"I...I..." Though I can't see her eyes, I can feel her stare. Her lips are still pursed, and I scramble to remember what she told us the rules of the game were. Oh right, if we like it, we thank her. If we don't like it, we apologize. Though I'm not one hundred percent on board with apologizing, I don't want to get hit with that crop again. It's not so much the sting of pain but rather her disappointment I don't want to feel again. "I'm sorry, Mistress," I say quickly. Her lips relax a bit, and one corner lifts into a sideways smile.

"Good boy." She reaches out her hand and rubs the spot on my thigh where she'd hit me. Her touch is soft and so close to my dick, I can't stop the rush of blood stiffening my shaft. An appreciative sound comes from her mouth before she looks back up at me.

"Thank you, Mistress," I say without thinking. Who the hell knew I had a damn praise kink? I bet Clarissa would laugh at the fact I even know what in the hell a praise kink is. My family would be scandalized, but Clarissa would laugh and then probably congratulate me. My lips quirk up with the thought, and Mistress Ingrid's head tilts to the side. My smile falls, and I shake my head.

"Your emotions seem to be all over the place, pet. Are you unwell?"

"No, Mistress. I am still working through my nerves."

"Do I scare you? Are you afraid I might hurt you?"

I shake my head and immediately say, "No."

"You seem to learn quickly." She looks up and over my shoulder at the other guys. "Much more quickly than your companions. Here is what I want, pet. You do not move unless I give you express permission or tell you to." She turns her attention back on me awaiting an answer.

"Yes, Mistress." Her smile returns and something flutters in my chest.

"When I ask you a direct question, you respond with words. No more of this nodding and shaking of the head. Do you understand?"

"Yes, Mistress."

"Now, tell me which of the toys you want us to play with."

I look up at the wall, though I already know my choice. "The one with the white feathers and thin leather straps."

"A little hard and a little soft, huh?" She asks quietly.

I smile. "Yes, Mistress."

Without another word, she turns to the wall and pulls down the flogger I described. A shiver runs up my spine as she caresses the shaft and then gathers the long strands in her soft hands. She walks around me, and it takes all my strength not to spin in circles following her. Suddenly, I feel it. The delicate caress of feathers against the backs of my bare knees. It's so soft, I almost miss the moment of contact. As soon as I recognize it, though, my body lights up like a Christmas tree. Coming around to my front, she runs the feathers along my chest until she stops in her tracks, reaching out a hand to trace her fingertips across my pebbled nipples. I hiss out an almost inaudible, "Thank you, Mistress." Her touch is as light as the feathers, and I want more. *Fuck, why hadn't I worn underwear?*

She drags the flogger up my chest and over my shoulder, making her way behind me again. Then she pulls it across my back. My breaths become heavy as my arousal mounts, and I want to groan like Travis had earlier. I won't do that, though. I wish she'd let me turn around to see what's happening with the other guys. I can't even hear them, though that might have more to do with how loudly my heart is beating than their distance in the other parts of the room. Are their mistresses being as gentle as mine? Has Travis done something yet to piss his off? Am I still the only one completely naked? I might not be someone who likes the spotlight, but I'm not ashamed of my nakedness or my body. Can Travis and Peter say the same?

I lose the ability to think when she brings the flogger down across my bare ass. This isn't the gentle teasing of moments ago. It stings and sends streams of electricity though my chest and straight down to my dick. She places her hand in the middle of my back and presses me to bend forward some. "Thank you, Mistress." Fuck, I'll thank her all day if she keeps the sparks flying. Once again, she runs the flogger softly up my legs before slapping the leather against my thighs and then my ass. I can't hold back a moan this time, which I follow up with more words of gratitude. *What the fuck is happening to me?*

"You're being such a good boy," she coos. My swollen cock weeps with precum at her praise. "Should we show the others what a good boy looks like, pet?"

My body and mind war with each other. My mind screams that I should keep this side of me to myself, allow it to be my secret, the fantasy I didn't know I had. My body, on the other hand, wants to be her good boy, to earn her praise and make her smile. "Yes, Mistress."

"Come, pet. Let me get you ready." I tremble with anticipation as she leads me to another area of the room I hadn't noticed earlier. She walks up to a wardrobe of sorts and pulls out what I can only describe as a loin cloth, except it's made of leather. "Would you prefer to be somewhat covered, pet?"

Her question catches me off guard. Everything I knew, or thought I knew, about dominatrixes came from movies. They tell you what to do and punish you if you don't follow their directions, but Mistress Ingrid does more asking than commanding. I'm not sure whether she wants me covered or uncovered. I'm also not sure how to tell her I will do whatever makes her happy.

"Don't make me wait, pet. I get twitchy if I have to wait. Do you want me to cover you?"

"Yes, Mistress. Thank you, Mistress?"

Her lip quirks up on one side as she grabs out a strip of soft leather, draping it around me and tying it around my waist. It barely falls below my ass, but she leaves it lower in the front, so it at least covers my dick, which cannot decide if it wants to be hard or soft. Instead, it maintains a constant state of mid-erection.

"Now for the last piece," she declares, grabbing a collar from the top drawer. I swallow. This somehow feels more demeaning, more intimate, more everything than even the flogging. She's been calling me 'pet,' and now she's going to lead me around by a collar like a dog.

The collar is about two-inches wide with a heavy buckle at the end and a ring on the front. It's heavy, and when she buckles it in place, the weight sits against my Adam's apple. I don't feel like I'm being choked, but it is hefty enough that the weight becomes a comfort in a way. When she connects the leash, I drift into a state of calm, and when she pulls on the leash, I follow.

For the next thirty minutes, she leads me between the other two pairs. Peter looks exhausted but satisfied. He and his mistress have fallen into a rhythm of give and take that seems to satisfy Mistress Ingrid. On the other side of the room, though, it appears that Travis has been flogged repeatedly and gagged since his mistress walked him away earlier. When we approach them, he has a ball gag in his mouth, and his eyes are red-rimmed but bright with silent excitement. Mistress Ingrid asks if he's ready to have the gag removed, and he shakes his head no. So, the next time he doesn't listen, my mistress removes the gag as punishment. I nearly laugh when he, once again, pouts like a petulant child. He really wants to be punished.

"Do you want to be naughty like Travis, pet?" Mistress Ingrid asks me, and I start to shake my head. She pulls on the ring of my collar with her finger, and I quickly add 'No, Mistress,' hoping my verbal response is quick enough. "No, of course you don't. What did I tell you good boys get?"

"Rewarded," I say in response. She smiles and strokes my cheek, still holding the ring of my collar with her middle finger.

"The thing all submissives must learn is that not all punishment is bad, and not all rewards are good." She turns her full attention on Travis' mistress. "One of the biggest lessons we must learn is how to tell when each is needed. It was easy to tell that your toy here," she reaches out and grabs a handful of Travis' hair, "came for the punishments, for the denigration. In giving in to him, you have rewarded his poor behavior. He has been the dominant one." She releases his hair and walks a few steps back. "There is not enough time to put this into practice now, but if Travis were to come back to you again, deprivation would be the best punishment for him. Does that make sense?"

"Yes, Mistress Ingrid," the other mistress answers. "I see what you mean."

"For my pet here, I can use rewards because he wants to please me more than he wants his own pleasure. Isn't that right?" She runs her hand through my hair, and I close my eyes for a second, savoring her touch.

"Yes, Mistress."

Chapter Sixteen

CLARISSA

When we finish the session, and I thank the men for volunteering to help with the training, Marc stands back away from the others, slowly pulling on his clothes. He approaches me after the other mistresses lead Peter and Travis out to the lobby, and I almost forget I'm still in Mistress mode for him. His dark brown eyes captivate me, and my hand starts to reach out and caress his cheek. I quickly pull it back and take a deep breath.

"Did you need something, pet?" I ask, putting my mask and accent firmly back in place.

"Yes, Mistress," he says calmly, a resolute look on his face.

"I don't usually indulge my pets once I've ended a session."

"It's just that..." He pauses, looking at me for permission, his puppy dog eyes begging. Curiosity pushes my better judgment completely out of the way, and I nod for him to continue. After a shaky breath, he blurts, "you said I'd get a reward." He blinks a few times and then finishes with, "I was wondering about the reward."

I can't help it; a smile breaks across my face. He's so

stinking adorable in this moment. I called him 'pet' as part of the game we were playing, but he truly is a golden retriever. Reaching out, I brush his dark hair back from where it has fallen over his brow, and he leans into the touch. Of course, I hadn't meant any additional reward besides getting what he'd wanted during the game. Who would have imagined that sweet, quiet, accommodating, and standoffish Marc Hart has a praise kink?

"What kind of reward do you think that good boys deserve, pet?"

He looks down and heat enters his ruddy cheeks. I might have missed it if I hadn't been watching him so closely. I put my index finger under his chin and lift it, making him look at me. He swallows. "I'd like a kiss."

The floor could swallow me whole, and I wouldn't notice. The building could burn down, and I'd be glued to this spot. I have been wanting to kiss this man for weeks now, and he has never once shown interest. Now, here he is asking me for a kiss. Well, not me. He's asking Mistress Ingrid. He's asking a character, a caricature, my alter ego. Tears threaten at the same time I want to rejoice. My fucking emotions are all over the place, and there stands Marc, my Marc, staring at me with hopeful eyes. It will haunt me for weeks to come, but I'm going to kiss this man.

I put my hand on his chest, pushing lightly, backing him up toward the wall. When his ass touches the spreader bar hanging there, I grab both his wrists and lift them over his head. He looks up. "Grab the hooks, pet." He does as he's told without hesitation, my beautiful golden retriever. "Now, be a good boy and don't let go until I say you can." He starts to nod, nervous wonder in his expression, but a quick brow lift from me has him answering.

"Yes, Mistress."

Only then do I reach up my hand and run it along his jaw,

my thumb rubbing across his bottom lip and pulling it down. My other hand wraps up around his neck, pulling his face down to mine. I stand there, staring into his eyes, sharing his breath, knowing he has no idea who he's about to kiss. His arms strain to maintain their upward position while I pull his face down, and with my heart cracking, I touch my lips to his. The kiss is soft at first, a simple peck that could be called chaste. Then he lets out a soft moan, and I'm lost, my tongue teasing his, my teeth nipping at his bottom lip. I barely stifle my own moan before I pull back to look into his eyes again. He simply stares at me in awe, desire swirling in his eyes so vividly, I'm surprised he hasn't pulled his hands down to take what he wants.

Voices from the hall break the spell. I use my thumb to wipe the saliva from under his lip and step away from him before giving permission to lower his hands. He drops his arms, flexing his shoulders a couple of times and twirling his wrists to bring feeling back into his hands.

"Thank you, Mistress," he says before grabbing his jacket and walking out through the door before my two trainees walk in to debrief the session.

I have to excuse myself to the restroom for a few moments to regroup. My mind is everywhere, and I can't even think straight enough to remember what they had or hadn't done well. I can't give them feedback when my body is on fire and my heart is out of rhythm. Earlier in the session, I'd known I wouldn't survive it unscathed, but I found myself breathing a sigh of relief at the end. Then he'd had to ask for the kiss he'd more than earned. He'd had to look at me with those pleading eyes. He'd had to moan against my chaste indulgence. *Fuck!* Why did he have to ask to kiss me now, here, in this costume?

When I get home, I follow my normal routine and call Marc as soon as I get in the bed. I'm not even sure what makes me call him, other than trying to pretend nothing has changed when I'm forever changed. Something inside of me says that he has also been changed because our conversation is very uncomfortable, like we have no idea what to say to each other. It's like our friendship has reverted to those early days when he wasn't sure how to approach me, and I used flirtation as a security blanket. Everything feels forced. I end the call before my voice exposes the tears running silently down my face.

Chapter Seventeen

CLARISSA

Time always seems to stand still after the holiday season ends. The week between Christmas and New Year's Day makes the flower shop feel like some desolate post-apocalyptic world. It's eerily quiet. The parking lot is huge and empty again. Carol and I even putter around each other in silence, cleaning out the holiday flowers and creating an inventory to begin spring orders. Most years, it doesn't bother me too much. I spend most of my nights out partying, and my days are spent recuperating, so the silence is welcome. This year, however, I almost can't take it. I come in late and leave early at least three days a week. Carol, thankfully, doesn't ask too many questions, at least not until early January.

"Why don't you come with me to Sunday dinner with Jackson's family?" she asks, breaking one of the long streaks of silence.

I've never been up the mountain before. Truth be told, I've hardly left Ardor Point since I was a kid, and we'd go on family vacations. As an adult, other than going to my job at the dungeon, I stick close to home, close to Carol and the floral shop where I feel accepted and safe. I still haven't told her about that job, especially not since I learned of her painful experiences with her ex, though I know she'll never judged me for my choices or hold them against me. She'll never make me second guess myself. With Carol, I've always been free to be creative in every sense of the word. That's really all I've ever wanted. So, when Carol invites me to visit the Branches mountain home, I'm a little unsure. I've never met Nick's wife before, but Nick sometimes looks at me like an oddity.

"Marc will be there," Carol says when she sees the uncertainty on my face.

"He hadn't mentioned it," I retort.

Not that Marc tells me everything he does every day of the week since he met Mistress Ingrid, but we talk often enough that he probably would've mentioned going to Sunday dinner with Nick. I know he's elated to still be working at the tree farm in the off season. He really loves the forest and the mountain. He also likes working with Jackson. When Jackson reconciled with his grandfather and decided not to return to California, Marc jumped at the chance to join their team full time. I'm not sure how happy his parents are about him not returning to school, but I'm glad he's still close, even if I don't get to see him as often as I had when he was at the pop-up shop before the holidays.

"Just because he didn't tell you doesn't make it any less true. What's up with you two anyway? You were inseparable a couple weeks ago."

I bristle at her insinuation that there's trouble in our relationship. "We both have to work, and it's not like we live in the same town."

She gives me a sideways glance, and my hackles rise more. She doesn't share all the ins and outs of her relationship with Jackson, even though we all had to live their ups and downs. That was more drama than I'd ever witnessed with Carol, and still, she doesn't want to talk about it. I also don't want to admit how much I want to go see Marc. I miss him. Having our late-night talks over the phone a couple times a week is not the same. I give her a big sigh before agreeing. I have to play it off, else she won't let the curiosity go.

"Oh good! I didn't want to have to make the drive up myself. Jackson will already be there, and I didn't want to close the shop for the whole day."

"Yeah. Yeah. I already said I'd go. You don't have to tell me you'd have rather made the trip with your boyfriend."

I catch her eyeroll and laugh. "Speaking of boyfriend, is he all moved in?" I ask, wanting to keep the attention on her.

"He has to go back to California still for the rest of his stuff, but I think he's procrastinating. I can't say I blame him."

"Really? Why?" As lovey dovey as the two of them have been these past couple weeks, I can't imagine him procrastinating making this move officially permanent.

She shakes her head. "It's not my place to tell his story, but let's just say he'll have to deal with Diane and his mother when he goes. His mom is a narcissist, and, well, you've met Diane."

I shudder at the mention of that woman. She's a real piece of work and gave me bad vibes from the moment she walked into their hotel. I'm genuinely surprised that Jackson would have been with a woman like her. Finding out that his mom is a narcissist explains it some, though. I know all about living with a narcissist and how hard it is not to get caught up choosing those same traits in others. Everything I've done since I was a teen is to try and break the cycle, or rather to keep myself from falling into the patterns my mother set for me. No one should have to deal with that.

"Why don't you go with him?"

"What?"

"Why don't you go and protect him from them? You

handled Diane beautifully, and from what I heard, you did a great job telling old man Nick about himself."

She falls silent, and I can tell she's mulling over my suggestion. I'm surprised she hadn't already considered the idea herself. It seems like the perfect solution. He shouldn't have to deal with that alone, and she wouldn't be here worried about him, making me crazy in the process. At least, that was the logic Marc had used on me when he volunteered to attend Christmas morning with my family. Though my mom had been on her best behavior when he came through the first time a week earlier, she totally went on a rant about him, my choices of friends, well, really all my life choices, after he left. I considered skipping out on the holidays altogether until he offered to be my buffer. I hadn't explained all the details to Carol, so she assumed mom had invited Marc as my boyfriend. If only.

Chapter Eighteen

MARC

The start of a new year has always been a struggle for me because while everyone talks about new starts and their resolutions, I've never seen anything significantly change from one year to the other. This year, however, feels different. So much has changed for me over the past year, especially in the last couple months. I stepped out from under my family's thumb, went against the grain, and found a job I really enjoy. I made new friends, which has always been hard for me. I found the girl of my dreams, though she rarely thinks of me. And I learned a lot about myself. So why do I feel like everything I've built is falling apart. Oh, because Clarissa barely talks to me.

Something shifted between us after Peter, Travis, and I went to that dungeon. Our phone call that night was awkward. We'd not had a painful conversation like that since that afternoon in November when we went bowling. Instead, it had been an entire month of growing closer to each other and learning each other's hopes, dreams, and fears. Clarissa was the most interesting woman I'd ever met, and I couldn't seem to get enough time with her. Though we'd text each other all day, talk on the phone most nights, and hang out as often as possible, it still wasn't enough. She made me feel like I mattered, like I was enough, and I wanted more. I wanted so much more. Then Travis and Peter dragged me to that fucking dungeon. I'd wanted to spend the evening with Clarissa since it was one of my last nights in Ardor Point, but she had other things to do. She seemed to have other things to do multiple nights a week. I didn't want to stay in the hotel alone, so I took the hour or so ride with the guys. If they had told me where we were going, I'd have declined, but they waited until we were already there.

Then, I saw her, Mistress Ingrid. She was fucking Glorious in her sexy-as-sin corset and panties set with thigh high boots, and her body was just the way I like them, thick as fuck. Seeing her reminded me of the first day I met Clarissa, and she had on that fucking mini-skirt and fishnet stockings that had me drooling. I was far too shy to say anything to her, unlike some of the other guys, but I'd be damned if I didn't dream of her that night and every night after. Mistress Ingrid had something else too. It was like she could read me. She knew I was uncomfortable, and she not only found a way to calm my nerves but then she pushed me to learn my needs. Within moments, she had me wanting to please her, wanting to hear her praise, wanting to feel her touch. I'd never wanted that from anyone before, except Clarissa, my best friend, the woman who only wanted to be my friend. By the end of the session, I couldn't hold my feelings in anymore. I had to tell that goddess what I needed.

I'd asked her for a kiss, a simple kiss. The kiss she'd given me was anything but simple. It made my dick hard and my toes curl. It made me want to curl up at her feet like the puppy she described me as. It made me forget about Clarissa, if just for a moment.

It didn't matter that Clarissa was just my friend. It didn't matter that she'd probably cheer with me for the rush I got and laugh at me for the kink I unlocked. Guilt slammed into me as soon as I saw her name on my phone that evening. Guilt as if I had cheated, though we'd never kissed. In fact, we'd only held hands when talking about family drama and trauma. What I would've given to feel her hands on my face and on my body, touching me softly, rubbing me, like Mistress Ingrid had done. I couldn't keep my thoughts straight, and I couldn't formulate words that night, so our phone call was painful. She seemed distant and uncertain, and I couldn't formulate words to explain what I was thinking or how I felt.

Two days later, on Christmas, Clarissa and I went to each of our family's houses to serve as a buffer. Though we had played the parts well and made everyone think we were a couple, as we'd planned for weeks, there still seemed to be this chasm between us. Sitting next to her with my arm around her shoulders was hard because I knew that it would all end as soon as we no longer had an audience. Telling the story of how our relationship had developed in little over a month was difficult because all I could think was how quickly it all went wrong. I couldn't get the kiss out of my mind or the guilt out of my heart. Since then, we've barely talked, and the whole reason I agreed to go to Sunday dinner with Jackson and Nick is because the conversation might be better than me silently stewing at my parents' house when they ask where my girlfriend is.

When I arrive, Nick and Jackson are out on the porch chatting. They each have a beer in hand, and Jackson quickly offers me one before inviting me inside to meet his grandmother. Mae Branch is the absolute opposite of Nick. She's tall where he's shorter, and her hair is perfectly styled, while his hair and beard are both wiry and all over the place. She's in the kitchen pulling out trays of baked chicken. There are multiple pots on the stove, and I can see a pie and cake plate sitting on the counter. I'm not sure how many people she plans to feed today, but she seems prepared for anything.

"Oh, Marc, it's so nice to finally meet you. My Jackson has told me so much about you. I hope you know how happy he is that you agreed to keep working for the farm."

"Thanks, Grams, just tell all my secrets."

"Oh, my boy, if I'd learned anything in all these years, it's to make sure the people you care about know it. You might not get the chance again."

Jackson kisses her forehead, and then she kicks us out of the kitchen. I smile at her. "I'm pleased to meet you, Mrs. Branch."

"You call my husband Nick, so you can call me Mae. Don't make me feel older than him," she says with a chuckle.

I walk outside, Mae's words playing through my mind on a loop. 'Tell the people you care about how you feel before you lose the chance.' They are beautiful in their meaning and yet painful in the context of my life right now. How can I tell Clarissa how I feel knowing that I kissed another woman? Do I tell her about Mistress Ingrid? Would she even care about either of those things? I take a long pull from my beer, trying to silence the thoughts and focus on the conversation between Jackson and Nick. The sound of tires coming up the stone drive stops everything because my heart freezes as soon as I see who is in the passenger seat of Carol's car.

Jackson hurries to the car, pulling Carol into a tight embrace as soon as she gets one foot out the door. "Are you not going to get your girl?" Nick asks from my side, and I feel my cheeks heat. Someone told him about us, about the fake relationship they all seem to think we have. My feet move down the few steps and toward the car.

Clarissa's eyes lock with mine, a question hanging between us. I put a smile on my face, trying to keep anyone else from seeing. I don't know why it should matter whether they know the truth or not, but it does. With these secrets between Clarissa and I already, I don't want to worry about anyone else's response to learning a truth that should have been obvious. Her brow raises in question, but then she also puts on a smile and gets out of the car. She's wearing her signature black attire, though she's jazzed it up with a shimmery silver and black scarf. Her hair is getting long and sits right below her shoulders. Her soft curls brush against the lapels of her coat.

I open my arms, and she walks into them without a word. Her hands snake around my waist, and I pull her in close, burying my nose in her hair. She smells like sunshine and citrus, which is totally at odds with this overcast, January day. "I've missed you," I say. It's true. I have missed her. It's almost painful the number of times I've almost turned my car toward Ardor Point rather than coming up the mountain in the mornings or heading home in the evenings. I just couldn't bring myself to do it, unsure if she'd want to see me.

She pulls away first. "I've missed you too," she says before turning her attention to the house. I could feel the truth in her words from the way she'd held me, but she walks off without another look in my direction. Her voice echoes through the clearing with a loud, "Hiya, Santa," and I close my eyes for a few seconds before following her onto the porch.

After the outside greetings are done, Nick invites us all inside for dinner. Apparently, Mae cooked enough food to feed an army just for the six of us. We all follow Nick toward the dining room, but Carol pulls Clarissa off into the kitchen. I hear Mae's sweet voice welcoming Clarissa into their home much like she had done with me. I wonder if she's heard stories about Clarissa or about the two of us. I wish I could hear their conversation. Though Mae seems to be the sweet, grandmotherly type, the protector in me wants to make sure she isn't judging Clarissa for her clothes, her makeup, or her size, all the things so many people have judged her for over the years. All the things that make her uniquely perfect. I let out a relieved breath when they all come to the dining room smiling and laughing, trays of food in their hands. Jackson and I stand to help put everything out on the table.

"Why didn't you call us to help, Grams?"

Nick is shaking his head before Mae even gets a hand to her hip. "Boy, I have been cooking, serving, and entertaining since before your daddy was born. I'm not so old yet that I can't handle a few trays of food. Besides, the ladies here helped me out. You didn't see your grandpa jump, did you?" Nick hasn't moved a muscle, but I'm guessing Jackson assumed the same thing I had, that he never offers to help. I've known plenty of men like that, my father included. They love their women, at least in their own way, but they believe in gender roles and will not cross those lines. Apparently, we...I was wrong about Nick. Mae probably reads him the riot act too whenever he tries to stop her from doing something.

Dinner is delicious, and the conversation flows smoothly around the table, though I notice Clarissa hardly says three words directly to me. Granted, I don't send many her way either. We sit right next to each other, and yet the distance between us is huge. I have to do something to fix this. Finally, Mae begins clearing the table. There's still quite a bit of daylight outside, so when Clarissa goes to help clean up, I grab her wrist. The surprised look she flashes me is like a dagger to the heart, and I nearly release her without a word, but I hold strong. "Take a walk with me when you're finished." She stares into my eyes for a few long moments before giving me a nod. I let her go, and she walks off, grabbing one of the pots from the middle of the table on her way out of the room.

Now, if only I can figure out what to say.

Chapter Nineteen

CLARISSA

Heart racing, I wonder at Marc's request. Why would he want to go for a walk in the woods? There's literally nothing around here except woods. We've hardly talked these past couple weeks. Hell, we barely even addressed each other throughout dinner, though we were sitting close enough for our thighs to touch. But his hug had felt so real, so warm, so right. I hadn't even thought twice about walking into his arms when he opened them. It wasn't about our audience or what they might think. It was simply about the need to be close to him again. And he smelled so good, like cedar and bergamot. How could I say no to his request.

"Grab your coat in case it gets colder while we're outside," he warns.

I slide my arms into the sleeves as we start down the steps of the porch. "Where are we going?"

"Nowhere in particular, just a walk. I'm assuming there are trails around, or else there's always the driveway." When I don't say anything, he turns to look at me. "You're not afraid to be out here with me, are you?"

"No, Marc. I'm not afraid of you. I've never been afraid of you."

He gives me a wan smile and grabs my hand, pulling me toward the path that leads around to the back of the house. "How have you been?"

"I've been okay. You?"

He heaves a deep sigh and opens his mouth to speak but then closes it again. Instead, he links his fingers with mine and slows our pace. He looks back toward the house, and I let my eyes follow the path of his. We're in the direct line of sight from the kitchen. I can see Mae at the sink washing dishes. Carol is standing near her, probably drying them. Marc pulls me forward again, and we descend a slim slope toward a gazebo with vines crisscrossed along the back side. He pulls me inside the structure.

"The wind is a little too much to just be out there walking around. This is at least a little protected with the vines."

"I'm sure its covered in beautiful flowers in the late spring," I say, trying to calm the beating of my heart.

Suddenly, he drops my hand and turns to face me directly. "I'm not good at this. I don't like confrontation or confusion or any of that, but I can't keep on like everything's okay. I'm not okay. I haven't been okay for weeks, and I don't know what's wrong. Forget that. I know what's wrong, I just don't know what happened. I don't know how to fix it."

I back up a step. He hadn't yelled, and yet I feel like he'd screamed his frustrations. The words echo through me. I've told myself he doesn't care that we aren't talking, that things have changed between us.

"I need us to talk to each other. I need this uncomfortable silence between us to end. I need my best friend back. How do we...I...make this better?"

A single tear runs down my cheek before I even register the burn behind my eyes. He closes the distance and wipes it away with his thumb, his hand cupping the side of my face. I shake my head. "I don't know. I don't know what happened." I mean, I know what happened. I know exactly when things changed, but if he doesn't know, doesn't realize, then I don't know how to make it better, how to go back to what we were.

"Can I tell you something? No, I'm going to tell you something. I just hope you'll listen."

I look up at him, my brow furrowed. He's never been so declarative with his statements. He's always asked, even when it's something he shouldn't need to. I cross my arms over my chest, not sure I'm going to like where this conversation goes, even though I know something has to give. "What?" I ask, my voice as devoid of emotions as I can manage.

"Okay, sorry, not like that. When I arrived here earlier today, one of the first things I heard Mae say to Jackson was how important it is to tell the people you care about how you feel." He grabs my hands again and pulls me to the bench that runs around the inside wall of the gazebo. "Those words have been rattling around in my brain for the past couple hours."

"What is it you need me to hear, Marc? You know I don't do well with weird, cryptic statements."

"I care about you, Clarissa. I've missed you, missed us so much. I know you only think of me as a friend, but you're so much more than that for me, and I've been miserable these past couple weeks."

"Wait, what did you say?" The blood pumping through my veins is so loud, I'm unsure I heard him correctly.

"What part?" He asks, confusion splayed across his face.

"The part where you know that I only think of you as a friend."

"It's okay. I'm okay with it. I'm happy being your friend."

I hold up a finger, silencing him from continuing to repeat himself into oblivion. "And the part you said after that?"

"That I've been miserable since we basically stopped talking?"

"No. What did you mean by I'm so much more than that?"

"Clarissa, I..."

"Please tell me."

"God, why is this so hard?" He looks at me, his beautiful brown eyes begging for understanding, maybe even forgiveness. "I like you, Clarissa. And before you say you like me too because you're my friend, I mean, I really like you. I've wanted to kiss you since that first time we went bowling, but you never seemed interested in me that way."

Without a second thought, I fist his shirt in my hands and pull him to me, pressing our lips together. I can't let the moment, the opportunity pass. I need to kiss him, as me, as Clarissa. I need to gauge his reaction to kissing me. Maybe it's fucked up to test him like this, but I need to know. I need to feel the truth of his confession.

At first, his body stiffens with surprise. Then he relaxes into the kiss with a sigh, his hand cupping my face. When his tongue dances along the seam of my closed lips, I say a short prayer of thanks to whatever gods are watching and open to him. He tilts my head to the side and deepens the kiss. Wrapping my arms around his neck, I jump into his lap. Without breaking the kiss, he readjusts the way he's sitting and then slides his hands down my back. I gasp into his mouth when he cups my ass in both hands and pulls me to straddle him.

My fingers make their way into his hair that has grown out so much since he first came to Ardor Point. It's so soft between my fingers. His hands tighten on my ass, rocking me forward and backward, I grip his hair tighter. He hisses, and I moan at the friction happening between my legs through our layers of clothing. Pulling his bottom lip between my teeth, I nip at it lightly, and he freezes. The change in him is instantaneous and jarring.

"Marc, are you alright? If you didn't like that, you can tell me."

"I need to tell you something, but that is not it. I definitely liked it. Can't you feel how much I liked it?"

I can certainly feel his arousal. He's hard between my legs, his bulge providing the perfect point of contact for the friction I need, but something triggered his response. "Did I do something wrong?" I ask, trying to hold my body still when all I want is to rub up against him like a cat.

He shakes his head and lets out a quiet "No."

"Will what you want to tell me ruin this moment for us?"

His hands slide up my back, settling on my waist, and he pulls me close, laying his head on my shoulder. "Maybe."

I take his face in both of my hands and tilt it up, so we can look into one another's eyes. "Then hold that thought for another day." He looks uncertain, like keeping the secret might cause him physical pain, and I almost relent. "I have secrets too, Marc. One day, we'll lay ourselves bare, but for today, I just want to relish the fact that you want me like I've wanted you."

His eyes widen like my statement is a new confession, like I haven't been pouring my feelings through the kiss. I lean back into him, lightly pressing my lips to his, trying to coax him to relax again, be mine again. "I've wanted to be more than your friend since that night we sat in the hospital with Jackson." Lowering my head, I kiss up his jaw to his ear and then pull the lobe between my lips. His arms tighten around me again. "You make me love me, and I've not felt that in a long time." He turns his lips in to kiss my neck, sliding them down to my collarbone. I continue letting him know how I feel. "And fuck if I don't wish we weren't out here fully dressed in the middle of winter."

He chuckles and nods in agreement. "We should probably go back in the house and get you warmed up."

"Oh, I'm warm, but not enough for what your touch is making me want to do."

He smiles and kisses the tip of my nose before his expression turns serious. "This isn't a game, right? We're good? You really want me as more than a friend?"

Once again, I put my hands on the sides of his face, so he can't turn away. "Listen to me good, Marc Hart because it seems I haven't been clear." He bites his lip, which nearly distracts me from what I'm saying. "I have been happy being your friend." He tries to tip his head down, but I hold him steady. "Look at me." He squirms for a second, but then his eyes fix back on mine. "I have been happy being your friend, but I have always hoped for more. I'm so used to men trying to force themselves on me that I didn't think you wanted anything more."

"Are you saying, I should have just pushed you up against the ball return at the bowling alley, and we could have been in a real relationship by now rather than pretending?"

"No, jerk," I say, pushing at his chest before I reluctantly climb off his lap. "It was your sweetness and consideration that made me want more."

"You think I'm sweet?"

"Sweet and considerate, like a golden retriever. You've gone out of your way to try and make sure I'm happy and taken care of. I just wish you'd have let me know what you needed to be happy."

"I don't think I knew, not really. But I've learned what makes me very unhappy." I raise a brow as I run my hand over my coat making sure everything is in place. "Being separated from you. The silence. The distance. The detachment. I've hated it all."

"Me too," I agree, lifting to my tiptoes to plant a soft kiss on his lips before I grab his hand and lead him back to the house.

Chapter Twenty

MARC

If I thought Clarissa was on my mind all the time before that afternoon in the gazebo, I was sorely mistaken. Her kiss is seared into my skin, and the memory has tendrils of need running throughout my body. Of course, the entire situation isn't as simple as us finally admitting we're interested in each other, want each other. There are still other factors pulling at my psyche.

That kiss with Mistress Ingrid is still there haunting my dreams, making me second guess the strength of my feelings for Clarissa. How strong can those feelings be when I still dream of kissing another woman? How do I purge that encounter from my mind, or at least make it nothing more than a pleasant memory that meant nothing? No doubt, it meant nothing to Mistress Ingrid. The woman was just doing her job. Yet, the way she responded to my request. The way she deepened the kiss. The way she sweetly wiped the saliva from my chin before anyone saw us. There had to be more to it for her too, right?

I need to get a grip. Mistress Ingrid is a fantasy. Clarissa's the real deal. Why then, did Clarissa nipping at my lip set off warning bells, reminding me that I had given another woman a piece of me? That's the part that I can't reconcile.

"Either grab that end of the trunk or move out the way, Hart!"

I blink a couple times before realizing that I'm standing in the middle of the tree farm next to a fallen pine. *What am I supposed to be doing?* Peter stares at me, his hands down at the base of the tree at our feet. Peter stayed on with the farm too, and it's nice to have a familiar face when I come out to help with the trees.

When Jackson first asked me to continue working for Branch Tree Farm, it wasn't to do manual labor. He'd wanted me to help with the books. He's great with management, which Old Man Nick has learned over the past few months, but he doesn't want to be bogged down with the baseline numbers, such as inventory, individual sales, order numbers, etc. Jackson prefers to focus on the big picture of building relationships with towns, stores, and different events that need trees in bulk. Peter, however, was kept on as an arborist because he much prefers to work with his hands, and he loves cutting down trees. I like to come work outside with him a day or two a week.

I pick up the tree where he had lopped off the top. I'm able to reach my arms around it and lift, the two of us having built up our strength during the Christmas season in Ardor Point. "Have you heard from Travis recently?" I ask as we haul the tree to the trailer he's attached to one of the heavy-duty Chevys the company owns.

"I talked to him last weekend. He mentioned taking a drive back out to the dungeon. Do you remember that place?" I nod my head and chuckle, unable to help myself. "Yeah, I declined. It was a once-in-a-lifetime experience that I want to leave as just that, once."

"I feel you," I agree. "I'm not surprised he wants to go back, though. He seemed like he was in his element there."

"Him? What about you, Mr. Good Boy?"

I let out a laugh much more vigorous than necessary, but I need to hide the discomfort at his use of those words in a mocking tone. "Don't be an ass! Just because I listened when she gave instructions doesn't mean anything. I wasn't trying to get my ass beat, and I damn sure wasn't about to enjoy having a huge ass ball strapped in my open mouth."

"Yeah, that shit looked uncomfortable, and yet, he seemed to love it," Peter says while wiping his hands on his jeans after we toss the tree onto the trailer.

"He's a damn fool. Anyway, I heard through the grapevine that Travis plans to come back to work for the shop when it opens again in November."

"Really? That's cool. Do you think Nick will send the three of us again with Jackson?"

"No clue. That would be cool though. It was a good time, and now we know what the hell we're doing."

"Right!"

The rest of the afternoon goes by swiftly, and I'm able to keep my focus on the work rather than my mind running away to the two women pulling at my heart. "It doesn't even make any sense," I say aloud to my empty car when we leave for the day. It really makes no sense at all that Mistress Ingrid has any place in my thoughts or heart. Was she attractive? Absolutely. There was also an air of mystery around her because I couldn't see her complete face. Her body, voice, and aura pulled me in. She was nice to me at the same time she took control. Then, my surprise praise kink made things even more muddy. The constant state of arousal was heady, and I wanted more. When I asked for the kiss, it was because I couldn't bring myself to ask for anything more. I definitely wanted more. None of that had anything to do with my heart. I barely knew the woman for two hours. I knew nothing about her except how much she turned me on. Lust was not love, so why the fuck could I not get over the feel of her lips on mine.

Before I realize it, I'm turning east at the base of the mountain, heading toward Turnerville. I don't know the name of the dungeon to be able to call and book a session, nor am I sure I can find my way there since I hadn't been paying attention when Travis drove us that night. All I know is I need to see her again, need to know if the feeling was real or just something left over from the session. Was there anything mutual between us? Damn Peter for mentioning Travis returning to the dungeon. Damn him for reminding me of how she initiated my praise kink. Damn me for wanting to hear those words from her lips again. I look at the clock. There's still plenty of time before Clarissa's nightly call. I can make it back home by then.

The parking lot is fairly empty when I arrive. The entry hasn't changed, nor has anything on the outside. In fact, there's nothing out here that gives away the type of business the warehouse holds. If you don't know it exists, you'll never find it. Inside, however, is a whole different world. It's dimly lit with soft music and opulent decor. They spared no expense on the design. I didn't notice before, but there's a staircase that leads up to a second floor off to the left side of the entry. The guys and I sat waiting with our backs to it. This time, however, I find a seat that looks straight down the dark hall.

My plan is to just book a session for another night, but the receptionist insists I need to book sessions directly with Mistress Ingrid. I offer to leave my name and number for her, assuming she's too busy to see me. Instead, I'm sent to the sitting room. My foot taps on the floor while I wait. Since I hadn't planned to stay, my nerves are getting the better of me. Not gonna lie, I'm afraid she'll see my name and refuse my session. She had called me a puppy after all. I'm not sure that most women want to deal with men who behave like dogs, but maybe I'm missing something.

I see when she steps into the hall. My eyes track her, and I catch the moment of hesitation when she looks up and sees me staring at her. They probably keep the hall as dim as possible to give the women a chance to see their patrons without being noticed. There's no way I wouldn't notice her. In mere seconds, she steps out into the room and approaches where I'm sitting. Again, she's dressed in black leather, but today's outfit consists of tight pants that look painted on and a pink corset that pushes her tits nearly up to her throat. Fuck if she doesn't leave me squirming uncomfortably in my seat. The woman is stunning, even if she doesn't look quite as thrilled to see me as I am to see her.

"What are you doing here, Marc? I did not have a session scheduled with you."

"No, Mistress," I say, trying to tamp down the heat crawling up my neck. "I came to schedule one and was told you were available to schedule it on your own."

She seems to mull over my answer and accepts it. "Follow me," she says, but instead of heading back toward the dark corridor, she walks toward the staircase.

"Mistress?"

"Did I stutter, pet?"

"No, Mistress." I quicken my steps and follow her upstairs.

Neither of us speak again until she closes the door of the

first room we come to at the top of the stairs. This room is nothing like the one we had been in last time. That was a huge, open room with many areas sectioned off by the type of equipment they held. I can't see any equipment in this room. Instead, there's a bed along the far wall. It's large but not quite the size of a king, maybe somewhere between a queen and a king if that size exists. The headboard looks to be wrapped in leather, and there are various decorative buttons with chains hanging from them. Beyond the foot of the bed is a round table with two chairs. Each of the chairs has a hole drilled into the middle of the seat. In the corner beyond the table is a tall wardrobe-like piece of furniture. It's closed, so I can't be sure what it holds. The possibilities have my heart fluttering. When the door clicks closed behind us, I turn to see an entire wall full of hooks in various locations, but rather than a normal wall, it's almost completely covered in mirrored tiles. I can see the bed and all the other furniture in its reflection. I can see myself in the reflection.

"You look nervous, Marc. You sought me out this time, so what has you trembling?"

"I'm not entirely sure, Mistress. I wanted to see you again. I just didn't know what to expect when that happened."

"What were you hoping for?"

"A conversation maybe. Another game? Just to sit in your presence."

"Another kiss?" she asks, her voice hard. This isn't the same way she'd spoken to me during that first session. Is she angry I interrupted her free time? Would she prefer I schedule a session for another day?

"Maybe. I don't know. I just can't stop thinking about you, that night, and that kiss."

"Then I did my job well, pet. We both played our parts well."

"What do you mean by playing our parts?"

"Anyone who comes here is looking for a fantasy, a game, that they play for a short while and can take home with them for when the real world is too much or too uncomfortable. They want a memory." I remain quiet, but I never take my eyes off her as she stands with one hip leaning against the table. "Some want the fantasy of being controlled, being told what to do and how. They want to have all the power taken from them until they are unable to make any decisions because they are tired of making decisions in their daily life. I'm not truly taking their power away. I'm not taking away their responsibilities. I'm giving them a memory they can slip into when they are overwhelmed."

"I understand that, Mistress, but I'm not sure what that has to do with me."

She chortles. The sound is so low I'm not sure it actually happens, but her smile says she finds my statement funny. "You may not have been the one to initiate the last session. You did not even want to be here in the beginning, but it wasn't long before you showed the role you wanted to play, showed the fantasy you wanted to live."

My mouth drops open. She's saying she could read me, but I'm not even sure I know what my reasons or needs were. "And what was that fantasy, Mistress?"

"You wanted to be shown and told that you were enough. You didn't want to be punished because you'd had enough of that. You wanted to earn someone's praise and be rewarded rather than ridiculed. I gave that to you."

"And the kiss?"

She takes a deep breath before answering. "It was such a sweet, simple, and surprising request that I indulged myself in the moment we had both earned." She holds out a hand and gestures to one of the chairs. "Sit, Marc." My thoughts reeling, I do as she asks, hoping she'll clarify her meaning because it almost sounds like she's saying the entire evening had been nothing more than an act. "You surprised me by showing up here tonight. I did not think you would come back to find me."

My eyes widen in surprise. Did she not think I'd want to come back? Did she not do this for a living and want patrons to come back? Somehow, I'm now more confused than I had been when she seemed unhappy to see me downstairs. "Why did you think I wouldn't return?"

"This is not your scene," she says matter-of-factly. "It was obvious from your response that night that you weren't aware of your desire for praise, and I'm happy you found that pleasure with me, but you are not the pay for attention guy. You're not the attention-seeking guy." She reaches across the table and takes my hand. Her skin is soft and warm, just like I remembered. "The men who come to me are wanting and willing to pay to have all of my attention on them and their needs. Even those with a praise kink aren't looking for my enjoyment. They don't care about making me truly happy. They just listen to get what they want. You, my pet, wanted me to be happy with you."

My stomach ties in knots. She's telling me everything I've thought each time I struggle with my memories of her, and yet I don't want to believe her words. I don't want to accept that it had all been an act. That kiss was something more, had to be something more. I can't be the only one replaying it in my mind daily. Can I?

"So, I will ask you again, Marc. What are you doing here?"

There's something in her voice I can't quite make out, and, once again, she leaves me wishing I could see her eyes. I can usually tell someone's feelings and intentions by looking into their eyes. "Can I see your face without the mask?"

She pulls her hand back away from me and sits up straight in the chair. I get the distinct feeling she wants to leave the room.

"I'm sorry, Mistress."

"No, Marc, you cannot. The mask is part of the fantasy, but it is also for my safety."

I nod. How absolutely inconsiderate of me to not realize there might be multiple reasons she hides her face. All the women's faces were hidden the time we came. It never even occurred to me that just because I know she's safe with me that she might not be with others. I stand. "I'm sorry, Mistress. I'll go now."

"Marc, whatever you are searching for won't be found here. Whatever you're scared of isn't here."

She surprises me by not saying anything more. I expect her to say that she isn't the person I need. Part of me wishes she would say it and put me out of my misery.

"Thank you, Mistress. I appreciate your honesty and not just taking advantage of my confusion. Thank you for the experience and the conversation."

"Be well, pet," leaves her lips, but they don't hold the same tone of certainty her other words had. Maybe it's my imagination, but she sounds worried about what I might do next. There's nothing to worry about. I'll go home and continue with my life. I'll wait for Clarissa's call and pour myself into seeing where that relationship goes without the concern that I'm leaving pieces of myself with someone else. I'll give myself fully to Clarissa.

Mistress Ingrid doesn't follow me out the door or down the stairs. She remains in the chair unmoving until I'm out of earshot at least. I stop with the receptionist and ask how I can pay for the time I'd spent upstairs. The poor girl looks at me like I'm crazy. She tells me the mistresses determine their own payments based on the types of service rendered. There's no way I'm going to climb those stairs again and ask how much I owe for the conversation. It had been crazy enough coming here in the first place over a kiss from a woman I didn't know who had been spanking my ass just minutes earlier. Damn, I must be some kind of unhinged fool to have pined over her for weeks, even after working things out with Clarissa. Without another word, I hand the girl a hundred-dollar bill and ask her to give it to Mistress Ingrid before walking out the door to my car.

Chapter Twenty One

CLARISSA

I pace the room, tears rolling down my face. I'm tired of crying over this man, tired of my emotions being tied in knots because of him. I thought that finally kissing me after dinner last weekend would've dislodged whatever was holding him back from me. Instead, I'm here in this special hell designed just for me where the man I want wants me but a different version of me. Him showing up here tonight was the last thing I expected, the last thing I needed. It had already been a shitty day, and finding out my client cancelled tonight's session after I was already here and changed didn't make it any better. To have the relief of a walk-in client become my literal hell was not on my list of things to do. Nor was breaking Marc's heart.

How dare he put me in that position? The fact I even had to explain to him that everything that happens here is an illusion, an act, means that he should have never been here in the first place. The more I think about it, the more my anger grows. Travis should have never forced him to come. I hadn't been lying when I told him this wasn't his scene. Marc is entirely too sweet and too shy for this place. My shoulders fall as I hold back the words *and for me.* He is too good for me. I will break him and turn him into something he isn't.

Without preamble, I cut my shift short, throw my coat on over my corset without even changing, and jump in my car. I don't have it in me to sit around and wait, and I don't want to just sit here and dwell on the swirling emotions. I'm a mess. I'm trouble. I need to get my shit together before I'll possibly be any good for him.

Thankfully, the house is dark and quiet when I get there. I don't want to run into my mother, especially not half dressed, and I sure as fuck don't want to run into my stepfather. I don't have the bandwidth to deal with him or his sexual overtures. Truthfully, I don't want to be here at all, and I'm not sure how much longer I can stay. It's about time for me to find somewhere else to live. It's time for me to put some plans in place.

After a quick shower and putting on some warm PJs, I climb into bed with my laptop. First order of business, get back into school. Classes are scheduled to start soon, and I still haven't registered. My one-year hiatus had turned into three, and my nearly completed biology degree looms like a shroud. There's no way I'm going back to finish those classes. I won't give my mother the satisfaction of thinking she's finally worn me down, that she has won. I don't want to be a doctor. My dreams go in a completely different direction. I want to create beautiful things. I want to make art and use flowers as my medium. The freedom Carol has given me all these years to explore my creative side helped lead me to this decision. Quickly, I press the link for the fine arts department and choose four classes.

I'm so deep into my schedule and determining how long it will take me to finish all the requirements that I nearly jump out of my skin when my phone starts vibrating. The screen doesn't have to show me who's calling; I already know. I leave the phone buzzing on the side of the bed and let out a sigh of relief when it stops. Less than five minutes later, it starts again. This time the buzz is shorter, so it must be a text. Then another call. He isn't going to stop until I answer. Swallowing around the knot in my throat, I pick up the phone, willing it to stop before I push the answer button. The universe must be on my side because the buzzing stops, and I'm able to shut the device off before it starts again. Marc has taken up enough of my time and emotional energy this evening. Tonight, I need to focus on me.

The door of the shop isn't even closed behind me when I catch sight of Carol racing in my direction, worry written all over her face.

"There you are! My god, where have you been?" I look all around, trying to figure out what or who she's talking to. She walks straight at me and grabs my shoulders. "I've been worried sick, Rissa. Where the hell have you been? You haven't answered your phone."

I pull my phone out of my pocket and flip it, so I can look at the screen. It's black. I tap it with my finger, and nothing happens. It shouldn't be dead. I put it on the charger last night before falling asleep. I tap it again, harder, and still nothing. Finally, I hold the two side buttons for a few seconds, and the white icon flashes on the screen. My eyes go wide. Memories of Marc's repeated calls and texts flash through my mind. I had forgotten to turn the phone back on before charging it last night. I look up to see Carol's brows furrow even deeper.

"I forgot to turn it back on last night," I say sheepishly.

The question I don't want to answer is written all over her face, and I cringe when it comes out of her mouth.

"In the decade I've known you, you have never once turned your phone off, Rissa, even when you were supposed to be in exams. What's going on?"

Before I can answer, my phone starts blowing up with all the missed texts and voice messages.

"How many of those are from me?" she asks.

I scroll down the screen. "Six."

"Your phone just buzzed at least fifteen times. Who were the rest from?"

"I'm guessing you already know," I say, my voice weaker than I want it to be.

My greatest fear is that Carol will one day tire of me, so I try really hard to never make her mad at me, or worried about me, or worse disappointed in me. For some reason, it feels like today will be the day for all three. Without another word, she walks past me, pulls the front door shut completely and flips the lock.

"There is something going on with you, and we're going to talk it out." I close my eyes, trying to stop the slamming of my heartbeat in my chest. She grabs my hand and pulls me to the back of the store, pushing me to sit down on one of the stools we keep behind the counter. "Now talk." I've always called Carol the sibling I never had, and now she's fully in big sister mode. It's always hot to see her take charge, and if I wasn't the one she was handling, I'd be cheering her on.

"What am I supposed to say, C? I was busy last night, and my damn phone was blowing up, so I shut it off."

"Now you know damn well, that is not the whole story. You shut your phone off because of Marc. What the hell happened? Y'all had grown a bit distant after Christmas, but you seemed to have kissed and made up at dinner the other night."

Heat rises in my cheeks at her use of that phrase. No one could've seen us in the gazebo, but still, the thought has me blushing. "I don't know what you're talking about. Will you please leave it alone?"

"No. Do you remember when that whole situation happened between me and Jackson? I spilled my guts to you. You, my dear, have been holding secrets from me, and I want to know what is going on with you. I can't help what I don't know."

"There's nothing to help. There's nothing to fix. There's nothing going on."

She takes a deep breath and lets it out. Hurt, worry, and anger stew just below the surface. I see it on her face and feel it emanating from her. Part of me wants to tell her, wants to lay it all out there and get some genuine advice. The rest of me says fuck that. I've always handled things on my own. There's no reason to believe I can't manage a brokenhearted boy, even if it means my heart breaks as well.

"You said you were working on something last night?" Her voice is softer and holds a hopeful note. I can give her this one.

"I was registering for classes. I decided it was time to go back and get my degree, but I had to work through the number of classes I'd need to finish a new major."

"That's wonderful, Rissa. I know taking all that time off has really been wearing on you."

I haven't told her that it isn't the time off but my mother's nagging and whining about the embarrassment of me not finishing my degree and choosing to work in a floral shop instead when I've had the whole world lain at my feet. Her words, not mine. I'm so tired of hearing her try and tear me down, trying to force her will, just so she can brag about her daughter the doctor, like I'm not worth anything now as her daughter. My sight blurs, and I blink the tears away, but I'm not fast enough for Carol not to catch the shift in my emotions.

"You're not happy about going back?"

I shake my head and then nod before shaking my head again. I'm afraid that if I try to say anything, the only thing that'll come out is a sob. I take a couple deep breaths and then clear my throat. "Yes, I want to go back," I say, my voice soggy like it's been steeped in tears.

Carol pulls the other stool closer to me and sits down on it, taking my hands in hers. "Honey, you don't sound happy at all."

My breaths come faster, and my chest tightens. Panic is trying to settle in, and I'm not even sure what's causing it. Carol won't hurt me. She would literally do anything to not hurt me. "I'm sorry. My...I...I'm all over the place."

"Rissa, talk to me. I'm here for you. Whatever is happening, I'm in your corner, always."

That's all it takes. Those last few words break the dam, and the tears start rolling. Within seconds, I'm sobbing chest heaving, snot running, sobs. I can't hold it. "I can't do this anymore, C. I can't fight the battles at home and then worry about hearts elsewhere. It's all just too much."

Carol wraps her arms around my shoulders and holds my head against her chest. She doesn't acknowledge my words or say anything, just holds me until the sobbing stops, and nothing is left but sniffles. Then she releases me and grabs for the box of tissues we always keep under the counter for the inevitable shopper with flower allergies.

"Have things gotten worse at home?" Her voice remains soft, but there's an edge to it.

So many times, she's offered to confront my mother for or with me. Each time, I brush it off. I don't want anyone fighting my battles. In fact, Marc had been the first person I'd brought to my house since high school. As if that didn't say what he meant to me. Another sob tears through me. I'm losing it, absolutely losing my mind. I almost never cry, and never over someone else. Why is this man under my skin? Finally, I shake my head, trying to focus on the conversation at hand.

"No. It's the same shitty mess as always. Mother continues to be more concerned about what the neighbors and her fake friends think than about me. Other than my stepfather being more overt in his intimations, things are just peachy." Though the sarcasm rolls off my tongue, it tastes like chalk in my mouth. My fucked-up home life isn't what's bothering me right now, but it's a much easier topic than Marc and our friendship/relationship/I don't know what to call it now that it's falling to shit too. "I just need to get out of that house."

"You know you're always welcome to come stay with me. I've been offering for years."

"I'm not your responsibility, C. If I can't figure out how to move out and live on my own, then I might as well stay there. I know that probably doesn't make any sense, but it's how I feel. You've done enough just giving me a job and being my friend." She shakes her head, ready to argue, so I try a different tactic. "Besides, I do not want to move in and listen to you and Jackson fucking like rabbits down the hall."

Carol rolls her eyes, and I smirk. She knows I'm right, and that's not a boundary she wants to cross. There's no way she's going to forego sex with her new boyfriend just because I need a safe place to stay. I know I wouldn't, especially not if I had someone as hot as Jackson Fucking Branch. *You could have Marc,* my asshole brain screams at me, and I shake my head trying to silence the voice.

"Fine. Home really isn't the issue then. So, what is happening with Marc that has had you in knots this past month?"

"You're not going to let this go, are you?"

"I'm not going to let you go. You are what matters, your happiness."

I bite my tongue to stifle another sob. "Dammit, C! Don't make me start crying again."

Chapter Twenty Two

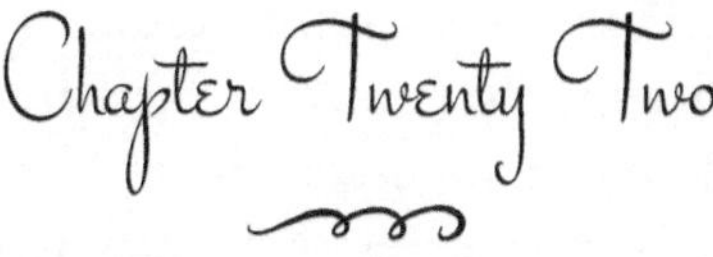

MARC

I can't seem to keep my head on straight. I'm supposed to go back out to the farm and work with Peter again, but I nearly let a tree fall on my head this morning because I couldn't pay attention. He sent me back to the office. The past three hours have been a blur of me looking at the same fucking spreadsheet and none of the numbers making any sense.

"Marc," Jackson says from the door, and I nearly jump out of my seat.

I look up to see him looking at me, concern etched into the lines near his eyes. Jackson is in his thirties, strong and attractive according to all the women who came into the tree shop during the season. They'd just come by and stare at him. Hell, he'd kicked things off with Carol like the first week we were there. The guy has some kind of chick magnet built into his ass, and he isn't afraid to turn on the charm. I couldn't have that much confidence if someone injected me with it like they were prepping a Thanksgiving turkey.

"Yeah, boss, what's up?"

"Let's walk."

I eye him curiously, cautiously, but then I get up from my

chair, close the files I've been working on, and follow him out the door. There are never many people here in the office, especially in the off season, at least not from what I've heard. One of Jackson's jobs is to run the office and determine staffing needs. That's one of the reasons I split my time between the office and the farm. Still, there are a few people in the double-wide trailer we use as the main office of Branch Tree Company. Jackson waves at the new receptionist as we walk by and pops his head into the office of his new marketing assistant. I follow in silence, nodding to the woman at the desk and passing by the open doorway without even glancing inside. Neither of us say anything until we're outside of the building and beyond the parking lot, heading toward the first rows of Douglas Firs that line the drive into the farm.

"Um, boss? What's going on?" I ask with an uncomfortable chuckle.

I've never had any reason to not trust Jackson, and it's not like he's got a shovel or some other kind of weapon on him. We walk another twenty yards before he starts talking.

"When I was a kid, we would only come out here to the mountain as a family once a year, either Thanksgiving or Christmas. My grandfather, Nick, would let me come to the farm with him and pick the tree for the holidays. We'd chop it down together. Me with my little plastic axe and him with his chainsaw. We'd take turns." I smile at the picture he paints of a young boy whacking at a thick trunk while an old man cuts through it like a hot knife in butter. Jackson isn't looking at me, just walking and talking. "One year, I guess I was maybe five, I asked him why we were taking turns when he could have just cut it down in seconds. Do you know what he said to me?" Jackson asks, turning to look into my eyes for the first time.

I shake my head. "No."

"He said that it was more important for us to work

together than to rush through and waste the experience." He puts his hand on my shoulder before continuing his trek through the trees. "That statement has lived rent free in my head for years, and it wasn't until recently that it started to make sense."

"So, what does it mean?" I ask him, genuinely curious because it sounds like one of them old-people sayings meant to get us kids to do something we don't want to when it really doesn't mean shit. It's like mental manipulation.

"It means that if we want something together, something meaningful, we both have to put in the work. But," he says, holding up a finger for emphasis like he's giving a speech to an audience. An audience of one, I guess. "But we don't all have the same tools, so we have to make space for each other to give as much as we can and then pick up the slack when we can without taking away the other person's autonomy."

I stop, mulling over his words and trying to figure out where he's going with this story. "Are you saying I'm not pulling my weight here? You're not happy with my work?" Had he heard about my near mishap this morning? Peter promised to keep that between us.

"What? No," he says quickly, walking back to where I'm standing. "This has nothing to do with your work here. I mean, it could apply, but you're using your skills and tools to meet the rest of the team where we are lacking. But it's also not your job that's had you upset, or at the very least distracted these past couple weeks, is it?"

I look down at my feet and kick around some of the loose pine needles on the ground. "No, it's not."

He smiles. "Who knew you and Clarissa would...I mean, we always guessed there was something between you, but it seems so unlikely."

"It wasn't," I say quickly. His brows furrow, and his lips open slightly like he has a question but isn't sure how to ask it.

I don't want to continue the charade with him. "We're just friends. We bonded that day all that shit went down with Freddy, but we've only been just friends."

"No way. Not the way you two look at each other. I could've sworn I saw you kiss her under an umbrella that one time."

I just shake my head. "No." I go to say more, but is there really anything more to say? I told her how I felt about her at Nick's house, and we made out like teenagers in the gazebo, but now she's ghosting me. How do I explain that to him?

"Tell me what happened between the two of you because I know what I saw after you all came back from your walk at Nick's house. That was not the look of two people who are just friends." He makes those ridiculous air quotes.

"We kissed each other. It was our first kiss ever, and it..."

"So, what happened?"

"I don't know!" I shout, more to myself than him. "Fuck, I don't know. Everything was fine before Christmas. Then I fucked up and pulled away. I think I just got in my head too much. We were friends, and I did something that made me feel guilty. It was stupid. So I told her how I felt about her at Nick's house, thinking we could at least get back to where we were."

"And?" Jackson's genuine curiosity spurs me to tell him everything. Hell, he already knew I couldn't get a hold of Clarissa because I made him ask Carol to check on her. I just needed to know she was okay. Then, once I knew that she was simply ignoring me, I'd lost my mind. Now, all I can do is think about what I possibly did to make her stop talking to me, but I can't come up with anything.

"So, now I haven't heard from her, and it's killing me."

It's nearly quitting time when Jackson and I make our way back into the office. He reminds me of his lesson about tools and meeting each other where we are, even if it's not halfway. I need some quiet time to figure out how I can possibly meet Clarissa anywhere when she won't talk to me. My phone vibrates in my pocket as soon as I close my car door, and my heart rate jumps. Finally, she's ready to talk to me. I pick it up and press answer without looking at the screen.

"Hello," I say, trying to keep the excitement from my voice.

"Hey, Marc. How's it going?"

My heart sinks. Travis' voice is the last one I expect to hear, the last one I want to hear, right now. I haven't spoken to him since we closed the tree shop. The only thing I've heard from the guy has come through Peter, as the two of them still talk regularly. It was that damn trip to the dungeon he insisted we take that started all the trouble between Clarissa and me to begin with. I sigh. It isn't his fault or even the trip. It was my fucking response to the experience that caused the downward spiral.

"Dude, you there? You okay?"

"What? Yeah, I'm cool, just shocked by your call after all this time."

"Yeah, sorry. I've been busy."

I nod silently, knowing he can't see me. "What's up?"

He takes a breath that I'm able to hear through the phone, and the hairs on my arms stand up. Nothing good can come from the need to stabilize that deeply. Finally, he asks a question I would have never expected.

"What's up with you and Clarissa? You two still a thing?"

It's dark in my car, so no one can see me, and still my eyes narrow. "Why are you asking me about that?"

"Look, I know we weren't close, at least not as close as you and Peter or you and Jackson, but I'd want someone to tell me."

"Tell you what?" I ask through gritted teeth. If he doesn't spit out whatever the hell is bothering him, I'm going to find and choke him.

"I wasn't sure how to tell you this, or what even to say because I know you hated it, but like I said, I'd want to know if it were my girl."

"What the fuck are you rambling about, Travis?"

"Clarissa. I just saw her somewhere I never expected to see her and thought you should know if you two were still a thing."

I roll my eyes and take a deep breath. I'm going to strangle him. "Dude, if you're not going to say whatever it is, I'm hanging up."

"Look," he says quickly, his voice filled with some strange emotion. Uncertainty maybe. "I came back to the dungeon for another appointment. I haven't been here since that night the three of us came. I was sitting in my car when Clarissa pulled into the lot and parked around the back of the warehouse."

My blood runs cold. I look around like someone's about to catch me doing something I know is wrong. I breathe in, but I can't seem to get enough air. I start the car and roll the window down. Though it's cold outside, I don't feel it. I'm already ice. Has she figured out my secret? Does she know?

"Marc, did you hear me?"

I hear his voice, but it takes a few moments before the words process. Another few seconds pass before I can breathe out a 'Yeah, I heard you.'

"You still okay?"

Why the fuck is he asking if I'm good? He purposely called

to tell me this shit. He didn't give two shits about Clarissa and me, or he wouldn't have dragged me to that dungeon in the first place. He damn sure couldn't have known how things changed between Clarissa and I afterward because I never talked to him. So, why is he telling me this?

"How do you know it was her?"

He lets out an incredulous laugh. "Really, dude? Like we didn't watch her get out of the same car every day for nearly two months? Well, we stopped watching so hard after y'all became an item, but still, the car was there. And how many other BBW goth chicks with blond hair do you know around these parts? It was her, man."

"Maybe she was just giving someone a ride. You said she parked around back, right?"

"Yeah." His voice changes again. This time he sounds almost apologetic.

"What is it?" I ask, needing, but not wanting to know. At the same time, I put the car into drive. I have no conscious destination, but I know exactly where I'm heading.

"I already had my session." He pauses, as if wanting me to put the puzzle together. When I don't respond, he sighs. "She pulled in before my session." Another pause, and the blood rushes through my veins, thrumming in my ears as if trying to protect me from what comes next. "Her car is still here. I didn't see her inside, but I think she might work here. I'm sorry, man."

I hang up on him. There's nothing else to hear and nothing else to say. Before we finished that first night, Mistress Ingrid told us that most sessions last at least an hour, though they can adjust the time for the client in extreme circumstances. If Travis had been able to check for her car without seeing her, she was inside and had been there at least an hour. There was a good chance she wouldn't still be there by the time I arrive, but I have to know, have to see.

It takes me almost an hour to get to the dungeon. In that time, Travis sends two texts apologizing. Then Peter calls, but I don't answer. I don't even bother checking the voicemail because I know Travis told him what happened. I pause a moment when I see Jackson's number come up, but he isn't going to change my mind. Right as I pull into the parking lot and drive around the back, a text from Jackson comes across the screen.

> Jackson: If what I just heard is true, do more listening than talking. You have the tools.

I'm not sure I have the tools for this. I spent the entire drive trying to make it make sense, trying to put the puzzle together. There are only so many scenarios I can come up with, and they all lead to the same logical conclusion.

Chapter Twenty Three

CLARISSA

As I finish up my session with Victor and Cameron, my new favorite couple, a knock comes at the door. We never interrupt each other's sessions, so something major must be happening. I apologize and excuse myself into the hall. That's when I hear the yelling. At first, I can't make sense of any words, it's just loud noise, but then the voice becomes clearer, and my heart stops. I don't even register who's at the door until Mandy wraps me in her arms and pushes me back into an alcove where I'm hidden from anyone standing near the end of the hall. I can barely make out Cale blocking the end of the hall.

"Hey, you can sneak out the side."

I shake my head. He's out there in the lobby, yelling both names. He knows. He knows and there's no way to pretend, to lie to myself that he'll never figure it out if I stay away.

"Honey, he's been yelling for more than ten minutes. He's not in the right headspace to talk."

Tears well in my eyes, as the next round of shouts ring through the hall.

"Mistress Ingrid. Clarissa."

I can hear the anguish in his voice. What everyone else hears as anger, isn't that. Not from Marc. He hates being the center of attention. He never wants the spotlight, and he damn sure has it now. I did that to him.

"How..." The words have barely started out of my mouth when the door to the couple's room jiggles. Mandy gives me a questioning gaze, and I shake my head. "Please," is all I have to say, and she pushes her way into the room closing the door behind her. I take a deep steadying breath and blink back the tears threatening to fall. Running my hands over my curves to reset myself like I do before every time I walk into the lobby, I put back on the mask of Mistress Ingrid. I'm missing my riding crop, which leaves me feeling more unbalanced, but I can't put off the encounter any longer.

Cale shakes his head when he hears me approach him from behind. He's trying to warn me about the situation, but I know this man. I know he's hurting and confused. I know he deserves an explanation. When Marc lets out an exhausted, "Clarissa, please," I break and tap on Cale's shoulder for him to let me pass. He turns his head slightly to look at me.

"Are you sure?" Concern etches every line on his face. I simply nod and give him a wan smile before stepping around him into the lobby.

Thankfully, there's no one else out there. I'm not sure if they cleared the lobby because of Marc, or if all the clients were already in their respective rooms when he arrived. Regardless, there's a strong likelihood the cops are already on the way. I have to get him somewhere secluded and quiet. I can't have them coming in to find him this distraught. They'll react first and ask questions after.

"Hello, Marc," I say in the best version of Mistress Ingrid I can muster.

He turns to look at me. His hair is completely disheveled, like he's been running his hands through it in every direction. Though he's been yelling and pacing, his face is pale. It's the look in his eyes, though, that tears me in two. He breaks me. His beautiful, puppy dog eyes, usually so eager, even back when he was still nervous around me, are lost. He opens his mouth to say something and then closes it again. Torment plays out on his face, and I swallow back a sob. I want to close the distance and wrap my arms around him. When he left here the other day, he'd been resigned. He'd accepted what I told him, and though he wasn't totally happy or on board, he'd accepted it. Now, He's here struggling to accept the truth I'd kept from him. Again, he tries to formulate words, but I hold up a hand.

"Not here. You've caused enough of a scene out here. Go upstairs to the room we were in the other night." He looks toward the stairs before turning his pleading eyes back on me. "Go, pet. I will follow you. I promise." The last part I say in my real voice. There's no use pretending anymore. Everything has gone to shit, and now it's time to pay the piper. I snort a sardonic laugh at the irony of that thought while I watch him make his way up the stairs, glancing down at me every couple steps. I keep the smile plastered on my face. *They don't call me the Pied Piper of Ardor Point for nothing.* A sob escapes the moment the door closes upstairs.

Cale touches my shoulder. "Do you want me to go make sure he doesn't leave the room before the cops get here?"

"No. I'd rather you didn't call them. Please."

He looks at me incredulously. "What do you mean? We don't wait to do that. They should be here any minute."

"Cale, please, no. He's hurt. I hurt him. It's a long story, but he didn't know who I was, and I don't know how he found out, but I know it's killing him. I did that. I'm to blame for all of that. He never calls attention to himself, never steps into the spotlight. I need time to talk to him, and then he'll go and not come back."

"There is no coming back after this."

"I know." My voice is weak. I know what he's saying is true. "Please don't let the cops arrest him. Let me get him to go home. I'll make sure he goes home."

"How can I know you'll be alright in there with him? The man was unhinged. Do you really think he'll be calm up there when he has you alone?"

I smile up at him. Cale is the man you want in your corner if there's any trouble. He takes good care of us here, keeps us safe, and now I'm trying to tell him to forget everything he knows to be true about behaviors like Marc's. I'm asking a lot of him. If things go south, he'll blame himself, but I trust who I know Marc to be. Unlike me, he's never pretended to be anyone else.

"I'll press the emergency button. Until I know he is completely calm, I will stay within proximity of the buttons." Cale's expression says he wants to argue further. "I promise. I will call if I need help, but I won't need help." He scoffs but doesn't try to stop me when I turn toward the stairs.

I stop outside the door and close my eyes. I'm not sure what we're going to say, what I'm going to say. I don't know how, or even if, we can fix this. *Deep breath, Rissa. You can do this.*

I don't know what I'll find inside, so I start off attempting to take control in case he still hasn't gotten himself in hand. "How dare you walk into my job and show your whole ass?" I say as soon as I step foot in the room. Marc is my golden retriever, and he wants to make me happy. At least that's what I'm hoping is still true. My eyes find him immediately. He's sitting at the table in one of the ridiculous chairs with the hole in the middle for strategic dildo placement. The scene would be a combination of comical and erotic if his eyes weren't so sad when they snap up to me. I see the conflict in them, the desire to hide away fights against the desire to rage at me, which is coupled with the desire to respond to the dominance in my voice.

Rather than the standard "I'm sorry, Mistress," he gave me multiple times the other night, he simply says a weak "I fucked up."

He could have said just about anything else. Hell, he could have done just about anything else. Screamed, cried, thrown things, anything. Those three words break me completely. Tears run down my cheeks and out from under the mask I'm still wearing, the literal one. The facade is already gone. I walk toward him and drop to my knees in front of him.

"No, Marc. I fucked up. Me." I take his hands in mine and look up at him.

"How did I not know?" He asks, sadness clear in every syllable. "How did I not see what is now so clear?"

My chin quivers. "I'm a good actress. I've lived my entire life playing pretend. It's how I protect myself."

"But it's so obviously you under that mask. That first night, as soon as I saw you come out of the hall, I was drawn to you. There was something..." He pauses. "I'd never wanted anyone like I've wanted you, Rissa. But then I wanted Mistress Ingrid, and I couldn't figure out why. I thought I was losing it. When you kissed me that night, I was so confused. I wanted her, you, her...ugh, this is so hard to explain. Even though we were just friends, I felt like I had cheated on you."

"I should have told you. I should have said something."

He laughs, but there's little mirth behind it. "I let you see me naked and aroused. I let you whip me with that flogger. I let you parade me around like a dog on a leash."

I smile at the memory. "Yes, you did. And you were completely, unabashedly authentic in every moment. It was beautiful. You were beautiful. I'm so, so sorry if finding out the fantasy was me playing a role ruined that memory for you." I stifle a sob. This moment isn't for me. It's for him. My feelings aren't important.

His eyes remain trained on my face for several moments before he shakes his head. "Can I take that mask off now? I want to see your eyes."

This is the second time this week he's asked me to remove my mask. Had I acquiesced the first time, we wouldn't be having this conversation. I wouldn't be waiting for the cops to barge in no matter how much I had begged Cale to call them off. If I had told him the truth the other night, we still might have ended, but it wouldn't have been like this. I nod and close my eyes, giving him control. I nearly hold my breath waiting for him to yank it off my head like one of those masks in the old Scooby Doo cartoons where the villain is just some basic person with delusions of being something more. The comparison is fitting. He doesn't yank it off, though.

The tips of his fingers brush along my jawline, and his thumb runs along my cheek until it's beneath the lace, wiping away the tears that have puddled right under my eyes. His other hand follows the same pattern on the other side of my face, and I wrestle back the urge to lean into his touch. *This isn't about me*, I keep telling myself. Once the fingers of both hands are under the lace, he slowly slides it up and off my face before pushing it from the back of my head. It hits the floor before I open my eyes to look up at him.

"There you are," he says. "You've always been there, haven't you?"

"With you," I respond with a sob, "yes. I had to play the role for everyone else's benefit, but I was myself with you."

"That's why you chose to work with me even though Travis was begging to be your test dummy." I nod. "That's why you sent us to separate corners when I had no underwear on." I nod again.

"I knew you wouldn't really want to be on display for demonstrations like that."

"Oddly enough, I'm not shy about my body. I don't like the spotlight, but that's because I don't want to have to act on other's attention. Still, that was considerate of you." I shake my head with a sad smile. I don't deserve any thanks because I tried to protect him while also lying to him. Lies don't warrant praise. "It was. As was the offer to cover me up when you had to go do the job you were actually supposed to be doing besides protecting me."

"I don't deserve praise for allowing you to maintain basic dignity. I lied to you. I hurt you. I could've told you that night and so many other times after. I could've told you at Nick's house in the gazebo when you wanted to share your secrets."

He laughs. This time there's less sadness in the laugh. It's closer to his dry wit. "Yeah, my big secret that wasn't really a secret when you already knew."

"Ouch," I say. "You wanted to tell me that you'd kissed someone else, that you had some kind of feelings for someone else." It isn't a question. I do already know. I knew that day, and I was too afraid of giving myself away to hear him say it.

"And now I want to tell you what made me want to kiss you then as much as I do right now."

My eyes go wide. Did he just say that?

"Yes," he says, reading the unspoken question, "I want to kiss you. But first, I want you to know why I asked to kiss you that first time." I stare up at him. "No one has ever pushed me out of my comfort zone while still making sure I was okay. No one in my entire life has put me first when it would benefit them to do otherwise. You did it that night with all the things we just talked about, and you're doing it tonight. I should be in the back of a police car right now. I have no doubt that the only reason I'm not in cuffs is because you're somehow protecting me. You could've left when you heard me calling you. I'm sure this place has escape paths, yet here you are."

Tears are flowing down my cheeks at this point. I don't deserve this. I don't deserve him. "So, who do you plan to kiss right now? Mistress Ingrid or Clarissa?"

He looks up like he's thinking about his answer before his gaze locks back on mine. "Both."

Chapter Twenty Four

MARC

I'm not sure what I'm doing, or why, but the drive to kiss her, to touch her, to have her has me wrapping my hand around the back of her neck and pulling her mouth up to mine. The hurt, the anger, the insecurity...none of it matters the moment our lips touch. Her eyes and her mouth are closed tight, like she's afraid to open them and find out reality is different. I nearly smile. This is the Clarissa I first fell for. The one who puts a show on for the public but is soft and uncertain on the inside.

"Look at me, Rissa. Be here with me." She opens her eyes, and I smile against her still closed mouth. "I need you to keep your eyes open. I need to know it's truly you and not some other persona I'm sharing myself with."

Her mouth opens. Whether it's with a silent gasp at my words or to respond with some argument, I don't care. I capture her mouth, plunging my tongue in to twirl around hers. My mind reels from the sensation of kissing her again that all I can think is, *please let yourself go, please let me in.* Finally, she does. Breathing a soft moan into my mouth, she presses into me, lifting off her knees, her hands clinging to my shirt. I reach down and grab handfuls of her thighs right below her ass.

She reaches up to wrap her arms around my neck and leans onto her toes, so I can lift her onto my lap. We melt into each other, hands roving everywhere. When she pulls my bottom lip between her teeth, I hiss and pull away from her, leaving us both panting. Her eyes are clouded with desire and uncertainty. She's still afraid I'll walk away.

"I have one question for you," I say, staring into her eyes. "How many men have had you in this room, on that bed?" It's a ridiculous question. I'm not even sure what makes me ask it, yet I need to know. I want to have her, to be with her, but I need to know what I'm up against. Sex work is her job, literally what she chooses to do. Can I even compete?

Her eyes open wide with shock and then soften with the compassion I've often seen on her face. When she finally answers, I'm not sure I hear her correctly. "None," she says, her tone as matter of fact as if telling me the weather. It's my turn to be shocked, my head tilting to the side. "Marc, I make my own rules here. I get paid to do only what I agree to. Do I get aroused by some, ok many, of my sessions? Yes. Do I fuck my clients? No. The most that has ever happened was when I'd let someone watch me get off. They'd often be tied to the bed or the mirrored wall there. The fantasy I fulfill is in their ceding control to me, allowing me to dominate them, to take away their choices for a short period of time. I did not take on the role of their sexual partner. Do you not remember that part of our agreement?"

I do remember her explicitly stating that there would be no penetration, and we were not allowed to touch the mistresses. "I assumed you meant because it was a training session, and we were in a mixed group."

With her head shaking, she reached up to cup my face. "That is my standard rule. The other mistresses were welcome to create their own rules outside of our training that could include whatever limits they had. I, however, focus on, and specialize in, emotional and psychological dominance that can also bring about arousal. I do not focus on, or promise, the proverbial happy ending."

I crush my mouth to hers. "I want you, Rissa. I've wanted you for so long, but I..."

"You were afraid you wouldn't be enough for me with all my experience." There's no condescension or accusation in her statement. Nothing but empathy comes from her lips. "Marc, you are enough. Even if I had fucked one hundred men, you would still be more than enough." She grabs my face in both hands, kissing my lips softly. "You saw me behind the facade I show the world. You accepted me in all my forms. You trusted me when I'd not given you any reason. And you're still here when I deserve nothing more than for you to walk out that door and out of my life." Tears burn the backs of my eyes, and I barely swallow back the sob threatening to escape my lips.

"Tell me what you want, Rissa. Tell me what you like and let me give that to you."

She stands, climbing off my lap with a smile. Without breaking eye contact, she works the clasps of her corset, dropping it to the floor once they're all open. My breath catches and my mouth waters at the sight of her full breasts. She's so fucking gorgeous, all curves and soft skin. With a smirk, she walks backwards around the bed until she can climb up onto it, never taking her eyes from mine like I'd asked her. My heart follows right along with my gaze. I'm so wrapped up in this woman, I can hardly think.

"Strip," she says, her voice sultry as she slides one hand over first one breast and then the other, pinching and twisting each nipple.

My heart bangs in my chest, and my dick goes rock hard. I pull my shirt over my head, breaking eye contact for the split second it takes to slide out of the collar. She's right there waiting, finding my gaze again as soon as the shirt slides off my head. I drop it to the ground and step out of my boots. Electricity sings between us, holding us like a tether pulled taut across the room. I unbuckle my belt and undo my jeans, pushing them over my hips, stepping out of them when they hit the ground. I don't bend down to bother with my socks. Instead, I lift one foot, nearly tipping over. A smile plays across her lips, but I refuse to lose her gaze again. I beg her to stay with me, so I won't be the one to lose the connection.

She lifts her hand and crooks her index finger at me. "Come here, Marc." I start to walk around the bed, following the same path she had taken, but she immediately shakes her head. "No. Come here," she repeats, using that same finger to direct me to climb up over the bed. "Crawl up to me."

It's like a sparkler goes off in my veins, tingling from the top of my head down to my dick. Yes, I'm an introvert. Yes, I'm shy at times. Still, I'd have never thought I was submissive. This woman, though. She dominates me and makes me want more. "Yes, Mistress," I respond with an embarrassed chuckle. Every damn time I'm alone with her, I learn a little something more about myself.

"You like being told what to do, pet?" I can tell the moment she puts back on the figurative lace mask. She almost reverts to full accent. It's like the best of both worlds having her like this, completely Clarissa with a hint of Mistress Ingrid.

"I like when you tell me what do. Only you."

"Then why aren't you up here on your hands and knees yet?"

I smile and put a knee onto the bed, lifting my body up to crawl toward her. She holds out a foot to my chest as I get close enough, and her head tilts to the side like she's trying to decide what to do with me. My heart pounds as I wait. When her pupils dilate to full capacity, I know she's decided. The look of desire and need has me ready to do whatever she asks. Hell, if she asks me to jump out of the window right now, I probably will.

"Kiss your way up, pet. I can see how much you want this body," she says, looking beyond her foot to my hard dick hanging straight down between my legs. "So, worship it."

She doesn't have to ask twice. I sit back on my heels, taking her foot in my hand. She didn't remove her boots, and it's so fucking sexy to see her in nothing but panties and these damn thigh high boots that I don't bother to take them off either. Instead, I kiss the tip of her boot before running my tongue up the side along her calf. Though she can't feel my tongue, it's obvious my actions are still affecting her in the way her mouth opens slightly. Her chest rises and falls, fluttering when I lay the one leg to the side of my knees and lift the other to repeat my journey of kissing and licking. Finished with that leg, I place it on the other side of my knees, opening her wide. I slide my hands up from her knees to her thighs, letting them linger once I get to touch her soft skin. A small moan leaves her lips, and my dick twitches.

Kneeling here between her parted legs has my body ready to go, but I want more. I want to finish her command. There's still so much more I want to kiss and lick and suck. Leaning down, I press my lips against the soft skin of her inner thigh, right above the top of her boot. First one thigh and then the other before going back to the first to lick at and suck the same spot, pulling the skin between my teeth. She whimpers and holds her breath. I repeat my actions with the other leg, and she tries to close her thighs.

My eyes bore into hers, and when I shake my head no, she lets out a shuddering breath. "I promised to follow your instructions, and you told me to worship you. I've barely gotten started." Her eyes widen, and I lean down, letting my body flatten onto the bed between her legs. I don't have a lot of experience going down on a woman, or up as the case may be, but the thought of tasting her, of giving her pleasure has me feral. "I'm not entirely sure what I'm doing," I say, trying to keep my voice steady. She gives me a soft smile. "If there's something you don't like, please let me know. And if there's something you want more of, tell me."

"I'll direct you if needed, but I have no doubt you'll make it good for me."

I drop my face to look at the way her panties hug her pussy, showing the lines of her plump lips. She's already wet, the evidence written in those lines. I press my nose against her panties, my forehead resting atop the soft mound at the top of her lips, and inhale. She whispers my name, but I don't have to look up to know that she likes it. Her fingers plunge into my hair and grab hold. The material doesn't have enough comfortable give for me to pull it to the side, so I run my hands up to the waistband and pull them down. She lifts her legs in the air to help, and I kneel up, peeling them slowly up and over her boots. I toss them behind me, to where my clothes and her corset lay on the floor. I tap the outside of her booted thighs, and she opens them back out on the bed.

My eyes travel up the length of her legs, along the curve of her hip, up over her breasts, and to her face. Nervous anticipation is written in her expression. She has nothing to be nervous about. She's absolute perfection, a goddamn goddess in the flesh. "You're absolutely gorgeous, Clarissa. I'm not worthy to breathe your air let alone taste your skin, but here you are laid out for me. I'm going to taste every inch of you," I say, unable to keep myself from talking. Once again, I grab her thighs and push them further apart, sliding my shoulders between her legs. I kiss the crease where her thighs and pussy meet on each side, listening to the change in her breathing with each touch of my lips. I make my way toward the middle, planting small kissing until I reach her slit. Opening my mouth slightly, I kiss the opening like I would kiss the lips on her face, teasing the seam with my tongue, and she whimpers again. The sound is like a siren song. I want more, and I won't stop until I hear her screaming like a banshee.

"Open her for me," I say, unable to control the need seeping into my voice. "I want to see you, all of you."

Chapter Twenty Five

CLARISSA

I'm already struggling to breath from the soft sensuality of his touch and his kisses. Then he goes and says something like that to me. Is it possible to get any wetter without actually coming? Geez. Before I can move, he's kissing down my slit again, spreading my lips with his tongue. He laps at my pussy from bottom to top, tapping my clit at the end and flicking his tongue along the tip. For someone who claims not to know what to do, he has me panting. A moan escapes my lips, and my hips involuntarily press up toward his face.

He pulls away, looking up at me with a smirk. "Which is it?" He asks, his lips glistening with my arousal. "Are you enjoying what I'm doing, or do you want something more?"

"Both," I say as I pull my lip between my teeth. His brow arches with a question. He's toying with me, wanting me to either comply with his request or tell him what to do. I want to see what he knows or can figure out on his own. Still, he has me feeling so good that I'm ready to give in to any request he makes. I slide my hands down over my breasts, giving them a squeeze, and then continued over my stomach. My fingers stretch out to pull at my FUPA, opening my lips to his gaze. His eyes watch me every step of the way, taking in every move and every curve until they lock onto my pussy spread before him.

Within seconds, and without preamble, he groans like a starving man and dives face first into my pussy. His lips and tongue devour me, latching onto my swollen clit and tickling the sensitive nub until I'm panting in rhythm. He gives no reprieve, not even coming up for air. His tongue slides down and pushes into my already wet hole. The sounds he makes has my walls clenching even before he begins pushing his tongue in and out of me.

"Fuck, Marc. Oh fuck. Don't stop."

He doesn't, and I don't think I could make him stop if I wanted him to. He's so lost to the moment. It isn't enough, though. It's the buildup. It feels so fucking good, but it isn't enough. I need more.

"Baby, use your fingers."

Moments pass, and I wonder if he understands what I'm asking for or if the message even made it through the haze he's acting within. Then he shifts, getting up on his knees slightly and rebalancing himself without taking his mouth off my pussy. He slides a finger inside me. I moan as he works it in and out.

"More," I beg. "Please."

He latches back onto my clit, flicking the tip with his tongue while he sucks on it at the same time that he pulls out slightly and pushes back in with two fingers. Yes, this is what I need, the friction that will send me over the top. He pistons his fingers in and out, almost hitting the spot, and I whimper again ready to whine about how close I am when he curls his fingers slightly, rubbing against my ridge. I explode in a sea of white as my body spasms. His name falls from my lips as if chanting to the gods. He pulls his fingers from my pussy and replaces them with his tongue, moaning as my hips buck through my orgasm.

His eyes are wild when he finally lifts his face from my pussy. "You taste so fucking good."

"Do I?" I ask, sarcasm dripping from my tongue in much the same way my release drips from his lips.

Earlier, only his lips glistened, but now, his entire face from the tip of his nose to his chin is glazed, and I want to taste myself on his lips. When he nods, his eyes hooded in satisfaction, I beg him to prove it. His head tilts in confusion at the same moment his mouth opens in surprise. I simply hold his gaze while he works through the request, making sense of my words. His eyes shine bright the moment understanding sinks in. He climbs the rest of the way up my body, kissing my belly pooch and then my breasts. When his cock sits right between my legs, I moan. And when he captures my mouth, I suck on his tongue, wringing the taste of my release from it before turning my attention to his lips. I lick along the edges and pepper the rest of his face with kisses. His fingers dig into my hips pulling on me as his pelvis pushes him tighter against my dripping center. I rub against him like a kitten, mewling with need.

"Lay on your back, pet."

He doesn't hesitate to roll off me and let my eyes take him in from head to toe. The last time I had him naked, I couldn't take my time enjoying the beauty of his thickly toned body. I had to try and remain somewhat professional all while aching inside. Now, I'm aching with the knowledge that I can finally have him. I'm no virgin, and I'm likely more experienced than Marc, but it has been a while, almost a year. Yeah, I flirt, and I work here at the dungeon, but none of that has led me to want a man inside of me. At least not until now. Now, all I can think is how much I want to feel Marc inside of me.

I run my hand down his torso, feeling his muscles contract

with every inch. As I near his belly button, his dick twitches in anticipation of my fingers gliding over the soft skin and hard length. He isn't overly long, but he is girthy. My fingers stretch to wrap around him, and his head is strong and swollen. My mouth waters for a taste. Dipping my head down to his stomach, I run my tongue around his belly button. He sucks in a breath. With his cock standing up straight, I repeat the movement around his tip, and he grounds out an unsteady 'Fuck.'

"Put your hands behind your head." As much as I want to suck him off and see if I can make him crazy enough to try and choke me on his cock, I want to taste him and then ride him like a seesaw.

Chapter Twenty Six

MARC

I've always hated asking for a day off. It's probably because trying to get my parents to let me do something besides work at their restaurant was a no-go. So, I've put off asking Nick for Valentine's Day off. I tell myself it would've been easier to ask Jackson, but he and Carol went on an actual vacation after coming back from packing up his life in California to move back here permanently. They were barely back a couple days before they took off to the Caribbean. The thing is I need that day off. First, I'm going to re-enroll in classes for business management. It's time I stop vacillating on what I want, thus giving my family the chance to wrangle me back into the family business. If he lets me, I want to help Jackson run the tree farm as a business partner one day. Second, it's Clarissa's birthday. She will officially be older than me for the next six months.

We haven't gotten the chance to spend much time together, so I want to surprise her when she gets out of her classes. We can go into the city and get some dinner or even try The Grecian Urn. Jackson told me that he and Carol enjoyed themselves the night they went back in November. Then, who knows? Clarissa's housesitting, caring for Carol's cat, so we might just go back to the house and watch a movie if she doesn't want to go out again. If I'm lucky, maybe she'll let me show her how much I've missed her.

"What do you need, Marc?" Nick barks from the back office.

He isn't a mean guy, though he had been an asshole during the holiday season, but he's gruff and sometimes a little scary. Jackson's secretary, who serves as Nicks assistant while Jackson's gone, gives me an apologetic smile. I shrug. I'm determined to spend the day and night with my girl.

"Today, Hart."

I nearly run down the hall at that second call. I'm not giving him a chance for a third. Nick is seated at the desk, staring at the computer screen, when I walk in.

"What I wouldn't do to go back to the days when we handled everything with pencil and paper. I calculated the acreage and the growth patterns of the trees, so I could predict the outcomes of the season. Now, I can't even figure out how to contact our damn irrigation engineer because I don't know how to use the damn email program Jackson has on this thing!"

"Can I help?"

I approach the desk slowly. This is not the first time I've had to help someone else with different tasks using technology. My parents really struggled when their accountant told them they needed to change over to electronic bookkeeping, and their vendors started requiring online orders. I had hoped that my skills would've shown them my value in the office, but they still insisted I help run the front of the house. They wanted to show off their son and say I was preparing to take over the family business. Not only did their insistence make me resentful, but it regularly broke my sister's heart. She was the eldest. She loved that damn restaurant, and she wanted to follow in their footsteps.

"I'll figure it out," he says, not looking around the monitor. "What did you need, son?"

I swallow. There shouldn't be any fear that I'll be letting him down by asking for the day off, but it's there nonetheless. What can I tell him that will make him less likely to think me lazy? I need to say something, but the words won't form on my tongue. *Shit!* After several moments, he stands and rubs his eyes, as if they're hurting. He walks around the desk, crosses his arms and looks at me directly.

"You look like you're ready to bolt. What the hell crawled up your butt and pulled your tongue down your throat?"

My lip quirks up on one side at the absurdity of his question. "As far as I know, nothing has ever entered that part of my body," I say with a smirk.

"Then why do you look so scared, kid?"

"That's a great question, sir."

"Nick."

"Nick. I need to ask for Friday off, sir."

He sighs and pinches the bridge of his nose with his thumb and forefinger. "Are you telling me that you're in here hemming and hawing because you need a day off?"

"I'm sorry, sir. I'd only ever worked for my parents before, and they didn't believe in taking days off."

Nick huffs a small laugh through his nose. "Life is short, Marc, too short. Unless we're in the middle of the season, which only lasts 8-10 short weeks, you're welcome to take a day for yourself. The farm will not fall apart if each of us takes a day now and then. Got big plans for Friday?" His eyes shining with interest. He, obviously, knows what day it is.

"It's Clarissa's birthday, sir, and I want to surprise her right after her classes end. I also have a personal errand I need to run in the morning." I don't know why I don't just tell Nick about my plan to go back to school. It shouldn't be a big deal.

"You really like that girl, huh? She's always been a showpiece."

"Yeah. I more than like her, sir. I just sometimes wonder if she's out of my league."

"She is, boy, but that doesn't mean she wouldn't be willing to join you in yours. My Mae was way out of my league, but she chose me, and here we are." His smile is huge as he talks about his wife. "Let Clarissa decide which league she wants to play in."

"That's good advice. Thank you, sir. Glad to know that anything is possible." I make to walk out the door before turning back to add, "And thank you for the day off."

He calls me back before I even make it to the threshold. He's finally willing to admit defeat and ask for help with the computer and email situation. I wipe the big smile off my face before I turn back toward the desk.

***The next scene depicts attempted animal abuse with the
potential for dire consequences where the MMC.
Though the scene shows more about Marc, you do not
have to read it to understand the rest of the book. Please
read at your own discretion.***

All week, I've wracked my brain on what to get Clarissa as a gift. Her family is loaded, and she doesn't want for anything except enough of her own money to move out without relying on them. I'm not exactly able to do that for her. I can barely afford the small single-wide trailer I rent because it's closer to the farm. I won't even consider inviting her to stay with me there, especially not when I know Carol has offered her extra bedroom already and been turned down. So, what to get the woman who has everything except the one thing she wants that you can't even give her?

I take the tight curves down the mountain, mind still wandering through possibilities, when I notice something off the side of the road that wasn't there when I made the drive up that morning. There isn't much of a shoulder on this stretch of road, and the nearest pull off is still half a mile down the road. I look behind me, trying to watch and listen for any other vehicle following me down the mountain. I can't let go of the uneasy feeling that something is wrong, so I turn on my hazards. There isn't much on this mountain aside from the farm and the Branch family house, at least not up this road. So, for something to just wind up along the curve is not only unexpected but worrisome. Making a quick k-turn, I drive the 500 feet back up toward whatever had caught my eye. The shoulder is a little wider on this side, and there isn't a blind spot. Any car coming up the road will see me first.

Grabbing the tire iron I keep in the floorboard, I put the car in park and climb out. I can see the top of something peeking over the ravine. There aren't any skid marks, so I doubt a car went off the road. Still, adrenaline pushes me forward faster. Whatever it is, the thing is made of wood and has a pointed top. It looks almost like a doghouse. *What the fuck? Why would there be a doghouse out here along the side of the road?* Then I hear it. A quiet whimper coming from the ravine, and I run toward the spot. *No fucking way. This can't be what I think it is,* I tell myself as I approach what is obviously a handmade, wooden doghouse. The roof of the small structure is red and reminds me of Snoopy's doghouse from those old cartoons. I almost smile at the thought, but another whimper freezes my heart.

The base of the doghouse is off the side of the ravine stuck between two small trees. I kneel along the edge trying to see inside the structure, but the opening is on the other side. My heart races. Though I'm afraid of what I might find if I pull this thing up, I have to know. I can't just leave it there. Thankful that I've continued to work out in the tree fields regularly, I stretch down and yank the structure up over the side of the road until it's settled on the narrow dirt edge. I turn the edifice around to look through the door, though I instinctively know it has no floor. The small house is empty. Why would anyone come up here and throw a doghouse off a ravine and not bother to make sure it hadn't gotten caught on the trees? Another weak cry comes from the ravine. With a lump in my throat, I crawl to the edge and peer over where the house had been caught between the trees.

Approximately five feet below the edge, wedged between the two tree trunks and the side of the ravine is a brownish ball. "What the hell?" I say aloud to the empty mountain. No sooner do the words leave my lips than two eyes stare at me from that ball, and then a tiny mouth opens, releasing a whimpery whine. "Holy fuck. Hold on, little guy...girl...whatever. Hold on!" I look around. The drop down here is at least 10 feet, except for where this puppy is stuck between the trees. I could maybe make the climb down, but if something happens, and I miss, or the trunk breaks, we could both fall the rest of the way. "Shit!"

"Hey!" A voice breaks through my panicked decision paralysis. I look over my shoulder to find Peter looking at me from his truck that's stopped in the middle of the road. "Dude, what're you doing It's not safe to be stopped on this section of road. No one can see you. What the fuck are you doing anyway?"

"Help me!" I call out to him, not wanting to walk away from the ravine's edge. The puppy is wiggling, excited at the prospect of being plucked from where he's stuck, and my heart is beating out of my chest with the fear of him wriggling loose and falling. Peter jumps out of his truck, leaving it running, and runs over to me.

"Dude, what..."

"Someone threw a fucking puppy off the side of the road and covered it with a fucking doghouse. Help me figure out how to get him."

Peter peers over the side of the ravine. "Holy shit!" He steps back and starts pacing. I learned months ago that these short back-and-forth laps are how Peter thinks through problems, but he's going to make me fucking crazy if he doesn't stop soon. "Hold on," he mutters and his footsteps head back toward the truck.

Without warning, the truck pulls straight toward me, my entire body in its shadow by the time Peter stops.

"Jesus Christ, man!" I complain when I realize his front tires are on either side of my waist.

Peter kneels with straps and cord in his hands. "Grapple down."

"What?"

"Let's strap you up, so you can go down there and get him. I can then pull you both back up."

I let him wrap the cord around me into a makeshift harness before he ties it off to the bumper of his truck. Without wasting any time, I begin the short climb down the tree. For me, that's an easier choice than figuring out how to use the cord for grappling. Instead, I let it be my safety net in case something goes wrong. As soon as I get within arms' length of the puppy, its wriggling increases, and I stretch out quickly to grab him, but I can't pull him free. Bile rises in my throat as I realize what's wrong. *If I ever figure out who did this, I'll kill them.*

"He's fucking chained to the tree, or else his chain got

wrapped around the trunk somehow. Either way, I can't just pull him loose."

"Shit, are you for real?"

"Yeah, man."

I climb down a couple more steps until I'm able to wedge myself in place and see what's holding him clearly. I hadn't noticed it before, but a chain runs from the doghouse down to the dog, and it's stuck around the small branches. The poor thing would have frozen to death, chained to his doghouse, hanging off the side of a mountain. Anger pulses through my veins, as I yank at the chain to pull it free from the limbs, snapping some of the smaller ones off completely. Grabbing the filthy ball of fur, I tuck him into my shirt. I need the use of both hands and arms to get the two of us back up to the top without depending on Peter's makeshift winch.

"It's alright, little guy. We're gonna get you out of here and checked out. Then I'm going to find the person who did this to you and throw them off the mountain."

He settles down along my waist, and I just pray where I've tucked my shirt into my pants holds. It's only five feet, but it feels like the climb takes twelve hours instead of the ten minutes it likely lasts. As soon as we're up on the road, I take my tire iron and snap the chain.

"You good, man?" Peter asks. "Is the pup okay?"

"I'm pissed, but I'll be better after I get him cleaned up and make sure he's not hurt. The poor thing is filthy," I say, pulling him from my shirt and inspecting him. When he starts shaking, I wrap him in my jacket, holding him close, and head for my car, thanking Peter who throws the chain and doghouse into the back of his truck for us to deal with later.

CLARISSA

I can't lie. This semester's classes are kicking my ass. Who knew that going back after a few years off would be such a difficult transition? The classes aren't hard, as most of them are just the prerequisites I'm missing from changing my major, but my mind is always wandering. I haven't gotten to spend any significant time with Marc since he found out about my second job. We'd had the most amazing sex, which, of course, plays through my mind at the most inopportune moments, like when we're drawing live nude models. I'm also tired all the time because of the two jobs and then our late-night conversations. Marc now understands that the dom gig is to help me get out of my parents' house. He doesn't like it, but he understands it, and that's enough for our relationship to move forward.

My professors are great. I'm especially fond of Mrs. McDermott. I took a couple art classes with her before as part of my general education credits, but I've been leaning on her more heavily since changing my major and having to figure out the best way to finish my courses. She's quickly become my de facto mentor and counselor. In fact, I'm almost an hour later than normal by the time I leave her office and head to my car. Maybe that's why I nearly jump out of my skin when a male voice calls my name in the middle of the quad.

I turn in a circle, trying to find the culprit. The voice sounds familiar, but it's too far away to be clear. If I didn't know better, I'd have thought it was Marc. He's working, though. The last thing he said to me last night before we got off the phone and went to bed was that he hoped to see me this evening for a bit. I won't lie and say I wasn't disappointed he couldn't make more time to see me on my birthday. Marc is a great guy, one of the best I've ever known, but I'm used to not being a priority. The fact he wants to come out and see me later will be enough. First, though, I have to put in a couple hours at the flower shop. Carol will not be happy if I leave it shut down completely on one of the biggest flower days of the year.

"Rissa!" The voice calls again, and this time when I turn, I find Marc sitting on a low wall in the middle of the quad where the walkways intersect. He waves, and I stand there dumbfounded. He doesn't get up or walk toward me. He just sits there as if he's a mirage. Do I just want to see him that bad? Am I just hoping someone will put seeing me on my birthday first? Tears well in my eyes, and my lip quivers. I barely register him standing before I turn away.

"Rissa, wait." His voice gets louder. "Hey, are you alright?"

His footfalls quicken as he approaches. I stop in my tracks. That's definitely Marc's voice, and I can feel the concern emanating from him. Turning around, I take him in. It's an uncharacteristically warm February day. He has on shorts and a t-shirt with a jacket tied around his waist. His naturally tanned legs are a warm taupe with barely-there black hair on the bottom half only. He's beautiful, and it takes me a moment to focus on the fact he's carrying something in his arms while he runs toward me.

As he slows down, the object comes into focus. It's a ball of fluff, a golden ball of fluff. My head tilts in confusion causing him to stop his approach mid-stride. He looks down and smiles.

"So, um, yeah."

He looks nervous, which makes me smile. For some reason, I love that Marc is never so cock-sure of himself that he becomes arrogant or condescending. He's my golden retriever through and through.

"What do you have there?"

"Can I say hi and kiss you first? It's your birthday and Valentine's Day, and I've been waiting out here for an hour."

"Oh my god," I say, clamping a hand over my mouth. "I was talking with my professor. We were trying to finalize my courses for next semester to calculate how long before I'd graduate with my new major. I didn't know you were coming." I reached out a hand, stepping closer to him. He puts down the ball of fluff and pulls me into his arms. "I'm so sorry you had to wait."

"It was worth it. You're worth it, Riss."

I smile and tears sting the backs of my eyes. "So, who's your friend?"

Heat creeps into his cheeks making them glow. "You know how you like to call me a golden retriever?"

"Mmhmm," I intone with a smile.

"Well, I found this little guy yesterday, and when I saw his color, I knew it was meant to be."

Again, my head tilts to the side. What is he saying? "Are you adopting a dog?" I ask, crouching down to offer my hand out to the puff ball at his feet. It sniffs my hand and then touches its little tongue to my fingertip before I rub the top of its head. "Hey there, cutie." It comes over and runs around my legs, bouncing a bit with each step.

"I'm asking if you'd like to adopt a dog with me. I can't

always be there, even though I want to, but this little guy could keep you company when I can't."

My eyes go wide. "You want to be with me? You want to raise a puppy with me?" As I say the words, my eyes narrow. "Or do you want me to raise the puppy because you can't?"

He holds up his hands. "Absolutely not. I'd never ask you to do something I wouldn't. It's just that when I found him, I was wondering what to get the woman of my dreams who has more than I could ever give her. Then this little guy caught my eye and stole my heart, much like you did." He reaches down and plucks the golden puff from the ground before putting his arm around my shoulders. "Just think about it. If you don't want to or can't, at least name him for me."

I eye him skeptically. "Marc, where did you get this puppy?"

He just smiles. "Let's just say, he dropped out of the sky." I can't help but laugh and shake my head. I'll pry the story from him later.

After I close the shop, Marc takes me out to the kitschiest bar and grill we have in Ardor Point, The Grecian Urn. The bartender who owns the place, wears horns and a toga. All the servers wear togas, and he has a singer who goes by the name Siren perform every weekend. It's ridiculous and yet a lot of fun. The drinks are strong, and the food is good. We leave the puppy in a crate in the back of the flower shop while at dinner and pick him up on our way back to Carol's. Cat-sitting Miel gives Marc and I a chance to spend some time alone.

We watch a movie on the couch. His hand traces up and

down my arm from shoulder to elbow as I lean against his side. The cat sits up on the credenza watching the little fluff with disdain while he runs in circles on the floor, playing with the couple of toys we bought him earlier. This is such a serene moment, emotion clogs my throat. It seems like I'm always in fight or flight mode, and I'm not sure how to handle the feeling of peace. Marc must notice the shift in my demeanor because he pulls me closer and uses the tips of his fingers to lift my chin upward.

"What's going on in that beautiful head of yours?" he asks.

I smile. If anyone will understand the uncertainty of the moment, Marc will. "I just...I don't know what to do with this moment." His brow furrows. "The serenity, the calm I feel here in your arms, watching TV and listening to the fluff play on the floor. It just all feels surreal."

"Ah," he says, kissing my temple.

"You're not going to try and explain it to me or tell me that it feels perfect because it is?"

"No. Why would I do that?"

I laugh and shift my body off him just as quickly as he tries to pull me back into his arms. "Thank you," I say and reposition myself to straddle his lap.

His hands go to my hips. "What for?" he asks with a knowing smile.

"For being you," I say, shifting my hips to rub against his already hardening cock. "For being here with me," I continue, running my hands up his chest and around to the back of his neck. "And for making me feel valued." I lean down and kiss his lips lightly.

His eyes sparkle as he takes me in, letting me control the pace of our intimacy. I reach down and grab his hands, pulling them up from my hips to cup my breasts. He groans with need and then pulls my lip between his teeth earning a moan. His hands explore under my shirt before a frustrated groan has him pulling the hem up and over my head. A satisfied smirk plays across his lips before I lean back down and covered them with my own. There's no rush tonight, no urgency. I just want to enjoy him, to have him enjoy me. As we kiss, I rock my hips back and forth, ensuring we both feel the friction between our bodies, stoking the fires that will eventually blaze between us.

"Rissa, I love the way you feel in my arms, on my lap, all around me. So soft and warm."

His hands graze up my sides, going back to my breasts, kneading them until my nipples harden. He pinches them through the lace of my bra before reaching around and working the clasps loose. As soon as he does, I pull the bra off my arms and fling it to the other side of the couch, pressing my breasts against his face. Without missing a beat, he starts licking and sucking between the two, his tongue grazing up my sternum until his face is buried between my heavy double Ds. He runs his tongue up my neck, kissing and sucking along my jaw while his fingers work magic on my needy nipples.

"Mmmmm fuck, baby. Let me feel your mouth on my nipples." Both of his hands squeeze my breasts together in front of his face, and he takes one hard peak into his mouth, lapping circles around it before sucking hard enough to make me moan. Then he repeats the actions with my other nipple. "Yes, that's it." Between his mouth on my skin and his erection pressing against my center through our clothes, I'm no longer thinking about taking things slow. I want him now.

Pulling back from him until my nipple leaves his mouth with an audible pop, I let myself slide down his legs to the floor. His eyes are hooded with desire when I reach for his belt buckle. Suddenly, he stops my hands, grabbing my wrists.

"Talk to me, Rissa. What do you plan to do when you pull that belt out."

I smirk. "Are you worried, I might use it to tie you up? Or

maybe you think I might turn you around and use it to beat you? Maybe you're not worried at all. Maybe you want that."

"No. Tonight, I want it to just be us. This is your birthday, and I am more than willing to please you. I want to know what you want. I love it when you talk to me and tell me."

So, I tell him. With explicit details, I tell him how I want to put his cock in my mouth and taste every inch of it with my tongue. I explain him how much I wanted the head of his cock to fill my throat and choke me until tears pour from my eyes. Then I want to climb on top and ride him like a fucking mechanical bull before I turn around and bounce on his dick like a pogo stick. By the time I finish telling him all my filthy desires, he's already unbuckling his belt, opening his jeans, and pushing them off his hips. His cock is at full attention, and I swallow to keep from drooling.

No sooner do I take him in my mouth than I squeal, pulling off him. His eyes go wide with surprised concern while mine fill with mirthful tears. Placing a hand on his chest to hold him still, I try to get a hold of myself. I reach around and pluck a little furball from the floor where he had been licking my foot.

Between laughing breaths, I give Marc a warning. "You might want to keep him up there with you before his little tickling tongue has me biting somewhere you don't want more than a light nibble."

He grabs the yet unnamed puppy, and I get to work making good on everything I said I wanted to do. He even throws in a few extra positions and a couple extra orgasms for good measure before we cuddle together in the guest bed. The puppy yips a couple times from the carrier Marc brought him to sleep in, and Miel hisses at him from across the room. Then, we all fall into quiet slumber, though my mind is anything but quiet. I can't fight the feeling that this is all too easy, too good to be true. With my body sated, my brain prepares for the shit to hit the fan.

Chapter Twenty Eight

CLARISSA

"Welcome back, boss lady!" I yell through the floral shop.

I have no idea where Carol is, but her car in the parking lot tells me she's here. Jackson took her on an actual vacation to the Caribbean, and I can't wait to hear all about it. She comes pushing through the swinging door of the workroom with a basket of clipped flowers in her hands.

"There you are," she says, as if I'm late.

Other than those couple weeks right after the holidays, I've not been late in the eleven years I've worked for her. In fact, I've been on time more often than she has these past few months, ever since Jackson moved in. Of course, I don't care that she's been late because this is the happiest I've seen her in all that time.

"Just because you showed up on time this morning," I say with a raised brow.

"It helps to be well rested," she retorts.

"You're trying to tell me Jackson didn't spend the whole week blowing that back out?"

She cuts her eyes at me, and I roar with laughter. Though she's not innocent at all, and neither am I, she always tries to feign shock at my innuendo. Okay, maybe I do manage to shock her occasionally. When she told me about the sexual escapades of young Carol, she didn't mention sexual talk or jokes. So maybe. At any rate, she should be used to me by now. As soon as she puts the flowers on the counter, I grab her in a tight hug. I missed her, and not just because I had to run this place all by myself.

"I missed you too, Rissa." She laughs and turns to hug me back.

"So, what did you bring me?" I cross my arms and tap my foot.

She laughs again and goes back to arranging the flowers on the counter. "How is it that I finally take a vacation after all these years, but you get a gift?"

I maintain my stance. "Because you love me. Because you missed me. Because this place didn't burn to the ground. Shall I go on?" I tilt my head to the other side.

Without lifting her eyes from the flowers, she tips her head toward the workroom. A smile breaks across my face, and I clap like a kid before rushing through the swinging door. I don't notice anything out of the ordinary at first and almost turn back around until I see the huge box on the worktable. It's so big, I mistake it for the tabletop at first.

"This huge box in here?" I yell out to the shop.

Rather than answer, Carol comes through the door, her face stoic. I stare at her quizzically until the corner of her mouth lifts. Only then do I take a tentative step toward the box. It's approximately six foot long by four foot wide and two foot deep. What in the world could she have possibly brought me back from the islands in a box like this. There's no way this fit on the plane.

"You didn't bring this back from your trip," I say firmly.

"Oh, but I did. I was on vacation, and I brought this with me today when I returned. Therefore, I brought it back from my trip. Just maybe not the trip you thought."

My eyes go wide, and my brain starts playing through all the possibilities. "Did you guys change your mind about the all-inclusive resort?"

She chuckles. "Not at all. We had a great time."

"Then..."

She cuts me off. "Just open it, Rissa. It's as much a gift as a proposition."

That statement confuses me even more. What kind of proposition is she making?

"Stop overthinking and open it before we get customers."

I look back at her, but she stands in the same spot, her face impassive. She won't give me a clue. Grabbing a box cutter from a stand to my right, I cut the tape holding the flaps closed. It's taped so well, I have to cut around each side and across the top. Whoever packaged this does not want it coming open. Carol still hasn't moved other than to lean against the doorjamb. I pull each of the four flaps open to reveal a huge slab of Styrofoam the same dimensions as the box. When my brows draw in, a small giggle comes from across the room, making me purse my lips.

"You're really enjoying this, aren't you?"

She shrugs but says nothing, so I turn my attention back to the box. Lifting the Styrofoam, I gasp, and my knees turn to jelly. I hold the slab so tightly that it cracks and with it my control. Tears run down my cheeks. *This can't be for real.* I pull the Styrofoam off completely and drop it to the floor taking in the full view. I run my hand over the sign before me. *There's no way.* I look toward Carol through the tears. She's standing across the table from me watching my face closely.

"Are you for real?" I ask, my voice choked.

"I have a plan for the future," Carol says. "Jackson and I

spent a good deal of our time talking about options for our future. I can't imagine you not being in it, but I can't just expect you to stay on as my assistant. I want to buy a small farm to grow my own flowers, and I want you to have a place to show your art. I'm hoping we can combine the two into a single creative vision."

She steps around the table toward me, and I'm frozen in shock.

"You are like a sister to me and the closest thing I will ever have to a kid of my own. I would be honored if you'd be my business partner."

"I...I...I" I swallow and take a deep breath. "I don't know what to say, C. Are you serious?"

"It's a yes or no question, Rissa. But please don't make me send this huge ass sign back."

The pleading look on her face makes me giggle. I look back down at the beautiful sign with flowers and paintbrushes around the new name C & C Galleries.

"What does Jackson think about this?"

"This has nothing to do with him. It was you and me before anyone else stepped foot in this shop. If you say yes, it'll be you and me here until the end."

My lips pull up at the corners. This is the Carol I know and love. Spunky, protective, and loyal. She'll never understand just how much I look up to and need her in my life.

"Let's do this thing."

"Thank goodness. Damn, you had me holding my breath!"

"It's called edging. Ask Jackson about it," I say with a wink and hug her tightly, not even waiting to see her turn red.

CLARISSA

"Good morning, C & C Galleries. Carol speaking. How can I help you?"

"C?" I didn't know who else to call. There's no one I trust more, no one I can depend on more. This is one of those times I wish I could walk up to my mother and be wrapped in a hug like I'd been as a young girl.

"Clarissa, what's the matter?" Carol's voice has raised a couple of octaves, and I'm not sure what to say. "Rissa, talk to me." My throat constricts, and my eyes well. "Honey, where are you?"

"I...I'm...I"

"Tell me where you are, Clarissa."

"At school."

"Where on campus?"

"Campus Health Center."

"I'm on my way. Give me twenty."

I blow out a sigh of relief. "Thank you." I'm so grateful I don't have to say anything through the phone. I also don't trust myself to drive. My head is all over the place. *Fuck my life!* I look around for my phone and remember that it was in the classroom with my bag and all my tools. I'll need to go back for them. With nothing more to distract my thoughts, I sit with my head in my hands, staring at the IV line running into my hand. How in the hell did I manage to be so stupid?

"Hey." A soft voice and light knock penetrate the small room. I look up into my professor's warm brown eyes. Mrs. McDermott has a tight-lipped smile, like she wasn't sure what she'd find when she came in the room. When her eyes catch mine, her smile grows. "I'm so glad to see you sitting up and awake. Do you mind if I come in? I brought your stuff from the studio."

I smile at her, trying to hold back the tears that are burning the backs of my eyes. "I'm so sorry for the disruption I must've caused. I'm so sorry."

"Hey," she says, rushing over to clasp my hand, "there is nothing to be sorry for. We were all just worried about you. I hope it's nothing serious."

Nothing serious. The look on her face says she just realized I might be seriously ill and contagious while she's here holding my hand. Nothing serious indeed. My entire life is about to go to shit. I can't talk to my mom, and the woman I look at as a big sister is barreling over here like a crazy woman because I couldn't talk to her. And my best friend is so busy between his own classes and working on the mountain that I haven't seen him in over a month. An entire month. Nope, nothing serious happening here.

"The doctor said I'm dehydrated." I lift my hand with the IV as if to say 'see'. "They said I can go home once they've pumped me full of fluids."

"Oh good." She sounds sincerely relieved. "Don't worry about Thursday's class. You worry about getting yourself well. I have no doubt you will catch up on your projects and far exceed expectations."

My lip quivers, but I quickly pull my mouth into a tight

smile hoping she doesn't catch the slip. "Thank you, Mrs. McDermott. I'm sure I'll have it all ironed out by next week."

She reaches up and gives my shoulder a light squeeze before asking if I have a way home. I tell her that Carol is coming to get me. She knows that Carol is one of the most important people in my life, as we've had opportunities to talk about her, the flower shop, and my plans for the future over the past few months I've been taking classes again. When the door finally clicks behind her, the tears I've been holding back once again run down my face. I don't need tears. I need logic. I need a plan. I need to talk to Marc. Realizing I forgot to ask Mrs. McDermott to pass me my phone, I slide off the bed and try to stretch the cords and hoses across the room to where she dropped my bag when Carol walks in.

"What are you doing? Rissa, what is going on?"

"I needed my phone."

She eyes the machines I'm connected to and her brows crease with concern. "Get back on the bed and then tell me what is happening here."

I chew my bottom lip as she puzzles through everything I've told her about Me, Marc, the dungeon, and how we are still trying to find our way with different schedules. I didn't even realize Marc had started taking classes again until a couple weeks ago when he mentioned having to write a paper. She can hardly believe we haven't seen each other the past month, especially after I tell her about him finding the puppy and offering to share him with me. Not that I can take him home to my mother's house anyway. That will never happen.

And now... tears threaten to fall all over again, but I choke them back.

Carol eyes me skeptically. "Um, Rissa, that's all well and good, but none of that explains why I'm finding you in the campus health center connected to monitors and an IV. What is going on?"

Just when I think I've gotten my emotions in check, she asks the question I don't even want to think about, let alone answer for myself. So, I repeat the same answer I gave Mrs. McDermott. "I passed out, and they say I'm dehydrated."

"That's all? Honey, I don't remember you being dehydrated before, ever. You're always drinking water or tea or something. Have you been sick, and I didn't know it?"

"Yes. No. I mean no, I don't think so."

She gets up from the visitor's seat she's been in and comes to lean a hip on the bed. "You just spilled your guts about months of lies, hidden jobs, and a fake relationship, but you're still going to keep more secrets? Why tell me anything then?" Tears fill her eyes.

"I'm scared," I admit with a choked sob.

"Scared of me? I hope you don't think I'll think less of you. There is literally nothing you could do to make me love you less, Rissa."

And with that, more tears run down my face, the sobs wracking my body until I can hardly breathe. Carol wraps me in her arms, holding me as I cry my heart out. Just when it seems like my life is coming together...

"I know you won't love me less, C. I'm just not ready for any of this. I don't know how to process what's happening."

"Let me help you."

I shake my head. "You can't. You can't fix this."

"Rissa, you're scaring me." She grabs my face in both her hands, forcing me to look at her.

Tears continue spilling from my eyes. "I need to talk to Marc," I say on a sob.

After watching her put all the pieces together, I see the moment understanding dawns.

"Oh honey," is all she gets to say before the nurse walks in and begins unhooking me from the machines, so Carol can take me home.

MARC

I check my phone again for what might be the hundredth time today. I've sent Clarissa at least ten text messages since this morning. Though we haven't had time to see each other the past few weeks... *wait, how many weeks had it been now? Fuck, had it been a month already? Dammit!* I need to make the time to go down and see her. Is that why she isn't answering my texts? Has it been too long, and she doesn't want to wait anymore? I might still hold doubts about being good enough for her, but one thing I know for sure is that Clarissa would tell me if too much time has passed. Once we agreed to try this thing as a couple, we also agreed to be open and honest with each other. She'll tell me. Won't she?

Before I can dig deeply into that painful thought, Jackson busts into the office I've been working in. "There you are," he says, a look of confused worry on his face.

My heart jumps into my throat at his expression. "What's wrong, Boss?"

"Get your coat." He takes a deep breath, looking straight at me but not really focusing on me. "I don't have any answers, so please don't ask."

"Boss, you're scaring me. What's going on?"

He shakes his head as if finally acknowledging me as part of this conversation. "Yeah, sorry. We don't both need to be freaking out for no good reason. Carol just text me that I had to come to the floral shop right now, and to bring you."

"Is she okay? Fuck, is Clarissa okay? She hasn't been answering me all day."

"I don't know, bud. I don't have any answers. We just gotta go."

I reach behind the chair next to me and grab my coat, leaving all my papers strewn across the table, laptop open and forgotten. All day, I'd had the feeling that something was wrong. I didn't know what, still don't, but I knew something was wrong. I should've jumped on that feeling earlier. If something has happened to Clarissa, and I could've done something earlier, I'll never forgive myself.

"I hear you thinking, and it's not helping my own anxiety, so please stop."

"Should I take my own car?"

"No. Carol said to bring you, so we go together." He bangs on the steering wheel as soon as we settle in the car. "Fuck!" My heart jumps again, much like it had the last time I saw him this upset months ago. I don't say anything, though, because I want to do the same thing. Finally, he starts the car, and we make our way down the mountain.

An hour and a half later, we pull into the parking lot of Carol's floral shop. I smile as memories of the holiday season seep in, but my smile drops just as quickly when I realize Carol's car is here, but Clarissa's isn't. She should be at work by now. Is Carol freaking out because she hasn't shown yet? Do I need to go searching for her? *Shit, I should've brought my car.*

Jackson is already heading for the door by the time I notice he's gotten out of the car. I quickly follow him, catching up before the bell can ding. The store is surprisingly quiet, which means Carol is likely in the back workroom. Still an uncomfortable tingle runs up my spine.

"Babe, you in the back?" Jackson yells as we enter.

The sounds of shuffling and falling boxes come our way, and we both take off running without a word. Jackson pushes through the swinging doors first and then stops so abruptly I nearly run into him.

"What the?" We both say at the same time. I step to his side, so I can see the chaos happening in the workroom. There are boxes everywhere, some folded flat, others ready to be filled. Carol looks up at us from the middle of the avalanche of boxes where she sits on the floor, tears streaking down her face.

As Jackson pushes his way through the mess, I can't hold back the question any longer. "Where's Clarissa?" My eyes scan every inch of the store and the workroom. She's not here. Carol sobs, and I stop breathing. Reaching a hand out to the nearest counter for support, I ask again. "Where is she, Carol?"

Several moments pass while Jackson holds her and strokes her hair. I want to scream at the woman in frustration. Her crying can only mean something's wrong, but she won't tell me what it is. She won't even look at me.

"Dammit! Where the fuck is she?"

Finally, Carol looks up at me with tear-filled eyes. Worry creases her brow. Worry and something else. Anger? At me? What the hell did I do?

"Do you love her?" Carol asks, pulling away from Jackson.

"What?" The question slips before my brain can even process it. Why is she asking me that right now? Clarissa and I haven't talked about love, haven't even discussed the future, other than our individual plans.

"Do you love Clarissa?" she repeats, her energy shifting.

"What's going on? Is Clarissa alright? She hasn't answered

any of my texts or calls today. I need to know she's okay." I pause. "And why do you look like you want to tear me apart?"

Her face softens, but her eyes remain determined. "Answer my question, Marc, and then I'll answer most of yours?"

Most of them? What the fuck does that mean? Why should I tell Carol how I feel about my girlfriend before I even tell Clarissa? Do I love her? Yes. I've loved her since that damn day we went bowling. I just wasn't sure she was ready to hear it back then. We hardly knew each other. Then that whole situation with Mistress Ingrid threw everything off kilter. We made it through, and somehow, I loved her more for her resilience and drive. But, again, it hadn't felt right to tell her when we'd just found our way back to each other. It's not something to send through a text message for the first time, or to say over the phone after a bout of phone sex. It's something to say at the right moment.

"I haven't even gotten the chance to tell her yet. It seems wrong to tell you."

She smiles then, though tears still fill the rims of her eyes. "That's good enough for me, but you need to tell her. She needs to know."

"Where is she?"

"She's at my house. She needs you."

Before I can open my mouth to ask more questions, Jackson tosses his keys to me. I don't bother to say thank you or goodbye. I turn around and run out of the store, starting the truck before I even close the driver's side door.

When I pull into Carol's driveway, the sun begins to set. It looks like there are no lights on in the house until I pull all the way into the driveway. Clarissa's car is suspiciously missing, but the TV glows in the waning light of dusk. She's here. I can feel it. Taking a few deep breaths, I get out of the truck and walk up the stairs, wiping my hands on my jeans before knocking softly.

My hand lifts, preparing for another knock when Clarissa pulls the door open, her eyes wide. I take her in from head to foot. She's dressed in My Little Pony pajamas, her hair up in a messy bun, and the remote grasped in her hand. On her wrist is a hospital-style plastic bracelet. I look from it to her face, and her eyes follow in the opposite direction. Not knowing what to say, but feeling a pit forming deep in my gut, I ask, "Can I come in?" After just a moment's hesitation, she backs out of the way, and I step around her, struggling to hold my hands at my sides to keep from reaching out.

Behind me, Clarissa closes the door and turns on the lamp before lowering the TV volume. "Have a seat, Marc," she says, her voice softer than I've ever heard it.

"I've been..."/"I've tried..." We both say at the same time. Then she gives me a wan smile and gestures for me to speak first. Before I can get caught up in overthinking, I blurt out the first thought that comes to mind.

"I've been so worried about you. So many thoughts were going through my head, and then Carol made Jackson bring me to the flower shop. She was crying. I thought. Oh god, I thought..."

I'm rambling. I know I'm rambling, but I can't stop. I take another deep breath, prepared to word vomit every emotion, every thought, every bit of my soul until it's all out at her feet. She doesn't give me a chance. She wraps me in her arms and pulls me tight against her until my nose is against the skin where her neck and shoulder meet. This time, when I take in a breath, it's to fill my lungs with her scent. The feel and smell of her wrap around me, bringing my heart rate down until I melt against her. After what feels like an hour but might've only been two minutes, I pull back from her.

Her hands reach up to caress my face, her eyes searching mine. Finally, she says, "I'm sorry I worried you." I start to shake my head, but she holds me still with her hands. "Let me talk before I start panicking."

Swallowing down the urge to tell her she doesn't owe me anything, I nod, and she releases me. The warmth that had seeped in begins to fade as soon as she breaks the connection.

"There are so many things I've done wrong recently." She grabs my hands in each of hers. "Please know that I would not intentionally make you worry. I promised to be open and honest with you, and I intend to keep that promise."

Her eyes look down at our clasped hands, and she presses them together, as if we're saying a prayer. When she raises that gaze back to my face, I give her what I hope is an encouraging smile. I should be freaking out at her pauses and silence, but I'm not. I trust her, and though I haven't said it yet, I love her.

She takes in a deep breath and lets it out slowly. "I didn't have my phone for most of the day. It was a rough morning, and I was running late for class. My plan had been to text you during our break, but I didn't get the chance. So much happened, and by the time Carol dropped me off here, I sat staring at all the missed texts and calls not knowing what to say."

Her gaze is filled with many conflicting emotions. There's worry, probably that I'm upset, but that isn't even an issue now that I know she's okay. Looking a little more deeply, I also find a hint of sadness. That emotion is a little more concerning, but it's the fear I see floating along with it that has me on edge. I look back down at our still clasped hands. Pulling one free, I run my fingers over the glaringly white plastic bracelet and twist her wrist over, so I can read her name and info printed on it. My eyes find hers again, a single question in them.

"I passed out in the middle of class today."

All the air leaves my body. Suddenly, my hands are all over her, touching her face, her shoulders, her arms. I run my fingers down her back, pressing a hand against her spine while listening to her breathing. There's nothing sexual in my touch. My body, my mind, and my heart all needed to feel her whole. I'm so focused on feeling her heartbeat and counting her breaths that I miss her calling my name until she finally shifts her tone.

"Marc, put your hands down and look at me." I do, instinctively submitting to her command. "Please listen," she says, her tone apologetic. "I'm here. I'm whole. I'm..."

I can't let her finish. "Clarissa, I love you," I blurt. Her eyes go wide, and her nostrils flare. I can't tell if she's surprised, scared, or angry. I put my hands up in supplication. "Sorry. All day, I felt something was wrong, and I didn't know what to do, but I had a feeling like you needed me. Then Carol asked me if I loved you before she'd tell me where you were or if you were okay, and I couldn't understand why. She said if I do, I need to tell you, and I needed to say it before you tell me that you're really sick and it looks like I'm saying it out of pity." I take her hands in mine. "I've loved you since that day we went bowling. I've loved every version of you I've met. I'd hoped to love you forever."

Her mouth drops open, and a tear escapes her eye. I wipe it away with my thumb before kissing the spot lightly. Then I apologize for interrupting her. When she opens her mouth to speak again, I steel myself for the worst news possible.

"Why didn't you tell me you loved me before?" she asks, her head tilted to the side.

I shrug. "It was never the right time, and I wasn't sure whether you were ready to hear it." As the words come out, they sound lame even to my ears. I'm preparing another, hopefully more eloquent, explanation, when Clarissa lets out a strained laugh.

"I'm not sure this is 'the right time' either," she says,

complete with air quotes. "You might change your mind when you hear what's really happening."

My brows furrow at the same time she raises hers in the way that screams she's about to drop a bomb, and everyone better be ready to duck the shrapnel. "For the record, I didn't go to the hospital. I was taken to the campus health center and treated for dehydration. While I was there, they ran some tests trying to figure out why I was dehydrated, after I told them I'm always drinking something." She locks her gaze on mine and worries her lip with her teeth before asking her next question.

Chapter Thirty One

CLARISSA

"What in the world made you think I was dying? I mean, I had a moment where I felt like my life was coming to an end, but not once was I actually dying."

"First, I didn't hear from you all day," he starts, his tone frustrated. "You just told me you passed out at school. You were in the hospital, no, the campus health center." He rolls his eyes because they might as well have been the same thing, and I knew my renaming the location wouldn't reduce his concern. "You're acting like you can't tell me what's wrong, like you're afraid to talk to me. Then, there's the fact Carol told me to tell you how I feel ASAP and sent me here. I mean, what in the hell am I supposed to think?"

"I'm not dying, Marc," I say without addressing his question. It's time to rip off the band-aid. "I'm pregnant."

Though I'm not sure how I expected Marc to react to the news, I surely was not expecting him to huff out a laugh. My hackles rise. I have been dying a little inside all day trying to figure out how to tell him or even what to tell him, and he laughs when I finally get it out. *What the hell?* Then, I look carefully into his eyes. His face is a big ol' ball of surprise, confusion, and relief. The laughter is likely from that last emotion, which makes my own relief bubble to the surface.

"I don't see what's so funny," I spit out, trying to sound irritated with his response.

"Are you serious? I came here thinking you were going to tell me you have a terminal illness. Babe, nothing else matters. You're here. You're healthy."

"I'm having a fucking baby."

"Okay. That's not a death sentence, Rissa."

"I'm having your baby!" I yell, my frustration at his nonchalance growing every second.

"Thank god!"

I blink at him. I literally just sit there and blink at him. What in the Twilight Zone is happening right now? I must look like a fucking fish the way my mouth keeps opening and shutting, yet Marc's expression remains awash in relief. I look around the room and finally manage a, "Have we entered an alternate universe?"

Marc takes my hand in his and smooths the other over my cheek. "Clarissa Litsyn, I love you. I wasn't kidding when I said it, and it wasn't conditional. You were the first woman to see me, the first person to truly see me and accept me with all my quirks. You mean the world to me. We already have a dog who misses you dearly, by the way. So, we'll have a baby too if that's what you want to do. If you don't, we'll make a different decision. All that matters to me is that you are alright. I need you, and I shouldn't have taken so long to let you know."

"Just like that?" I ask. My incredulity is a physical entity spreading out between us. "It's just that easy for you? You don't care about what this means and how our lives will change? You're ready for all that?"

"If you're asking if I was planning this, like I have my life in order, then no, I don't. Am I ready for everything it means to be a father? No, probably not, but who the hell is? Rissa, it's not that I don't care about the baby, or what it will do to our lives and our plans. I simply mean that if the two options I had today was to find out we made a life or that you would be leaving my life, then sign me up to be unprepared father of the year!"

"I don't understand you at all. Do you know that?" I grab his face with both my hands and kiss his lips, pouring all my love and relief into him. When he kisses me back, he takes my fear and worry too.

"Yes, you do. I'll panic later. I'll make you crazy, worrying over you and the baby every day. There will be plenty of that, but more than that, I will love you through it all."

"Dammit, why'd you have to go and make me cry again?" I bury my face in his shirt, basking in his scent, wanting to crawl into his skin. Instead, I settle for crawling into his lap. He kisses my head and my temple before wrapping his arms around me. "I love you, Marc. I have for so long, but I didn't want to ruin your life when you were just getting it started."

With his forefinger, he tips my face up to his. "You couldn't ruin my life unless you left it. You are the reason I breathe. Is our timing great? Well, no. Wait, what was our timing? Never mind, it doesn't matter. Just like me waiting to tell you how I've felt, there is no perfect timing."

"Do you really think we can do this? We're both in school. We both have jobs we love. We're just really starting this relationship, and we hardly get to see each other."

He kisses me before I can ramble any further. "We have time to make decisions, and we will. First, though, let me take you home."

"I told you Carol was letting me stay here until I have enough money for my own place."

He kisses me again, and with another roll of his eyes, he clarifies, "Come home with me tonight. We have a puppy to check on and lots to talk about. Not to mention the fact that I've missed you."

He says the last part with a wink, shifting under me until I feel his hard length pressing into my ass, and heat blossoms in my core. I've missed him too, and I've spent most of the day afraid I'd never get the chance to show him just how much ever again. The fact that he insists he loves me and still wants me, even with the possibility of a difficult future together kindles a spark of hope. No matter what decision we make about this baby, we have a future together.

Epilogue

Marc

Two Years Later...

We're late getting to the Cole County Lumberjack Showcase. We should've had these trees here two days earlier, but Jackson and Nick couldn't decide which ones or how many to send. Finally, I had to step between them and tell them what Peter and I had already decided as we walked through the fields looking at this year's harvest. I'm the expert in the farm's inventory, and he knows the health of the trees. The look on both of their faces when I said the truck had been loaded for two days had me rolling my eyes.

If this were a normal delivery, I wouldn't have cared how long they argued, but Clarissa was already in Carruthersville on behalf of C&C Galleries. I had hoped to be there to help her set up her vendor tent. Not to mention the fact that I now hated sleeping alone. She'd moved in with me over a year and a half ago, not caring that she'd gone from a mansion to a trailer. Six months later, Jackson and Carol bought their own farm, and Carol signed her house over to Clarissa. We've done some remodeling, making the house ours, and now I hate being in our bed without her there.

The moment we arrive, I leave Peter with the truck sitting in the middle of the concourse and go to find my girl. He shakes his head at me, but I don't care. He knows all about Clarissa and me, so it shouldn't be a surprise she's my priority.

Making my way through the vendor area, I spot a tent surrounded by potted poinsettias. The tent itself has been painted with large, colorful flowers of various varieties. I smile with the knowledge that my talented girlfriend was the one to make that plain white tent beautiful. I also know that her art, those created with real flowers and those painted, adorn most of the inside. My chest bursts with love and pride.

I sneak a peek around the corner of the tent before showing my face. It's quiet, and Clarissa's back is to me. Though I have the urge to walk up and wrap my arms around her from behind, I have no desire to bleed out from the boxcutter she always carries in the apron she's wearing.

"I almost expected to see a line of men from the parking lot to this tent when I got here."

"The Pied Piper of Ardor Point retired two years ago," she says, and I smile at the jab.

I know exactly what day it is, but I'll let her have her moment. "Has it been two years already?" I ask, pressing up against her from behind like I wanted to do when I first saw her. I might still be an introvert and socially awkward, but this woman can have me putting on public displays any time of the day or night. I put my nose to her hair and inhale, her scent rushing through my body like an electric jolt straight to my dick.

"Excuse me, sir, but we're not open," she says, and I finish her sentence with a quiet 'yet' as I tug on her earlobe with my teeth. I'm rewarded with a soft moan as she leans back into my arms.

"What can a guy like me do to get a woman like you to open up?" Her chuckle quickly changes to another small moan when I run my tongue down her neck.

"That's a good start, but if you wake either of the sleeping angels behind the counter, this woman will shut up like a clam."

With a smile, I step away from her and peer over the top of the counter she has set up near the rear of the tent. In the pack and play set up out of view sleeps a beautiful blonde toddler with soft chubby cheeks and a golden labradoodle. Lucky opens one eye, looks up at me, and gives his tail a couple of quick wags before laying his head across the baby's sleeping back. Knowing that our daughter is oblivious and well-protected, I return to my initial plan of action.

I step back over to Clarissa and pull her behind the curtain that's hung to separate the public space from the area behind the counter. As soon as we're out of view from the outside, I turn her to face me. She does so without protest.

"I've missed you," I say while running my hands down over her breasts, listening to her sigh as her nipples stiffen at my touch. When she opens her mouth to say something in response, I cover it with my own, letting my tongue intrude through the space between her lips. I'm rewarded with another moan. Her hands wrap around my neck and fist in my hair. As soon as she tightens her grip, I know she's on board.

With a quick glance down at the sleeping child, I turn

Clarissa around. "Grab the edge of the counter," I say. She may be the more dominant one of us two, but I sometimes take charge. I slide my hands beneath her apron, one up to tease her nipple and the other down into the waistband of her leggings. "If I were a gambling man, I'd bet that you're already wet." She huffs but doesn't argue. "I'll take that as a win."

My hand travels lower, cupping her fat pussy, my middle finger rubbing up and down the front of her panties until they're indented at the line of her slit. When I press the material between her lips, pushing my finger a little harder against her, she moans my name.

"Shhh beautiful. You'll wake the babies, and then I'll have to punish you by making you wait until tonight for your orgasm."

"Marc," she whisper-yells. "You wouldn't dare. You enjoy getting me off too much."

I push her panties to the side, saying "This is true, but we both know that little girl runs this family. So, try to keep quiet while..." I plan to say more but I'm lost in the feel of her when my fingers slide into her soaked pussy. She lets out a gasp, and I put my other hand over her mouth as I work my fingers in an out. "Fuck, Rissa, I knew you would be wet for me, but damn."

"I've missed you too," she pants out, and I can hear the smile in her voice.

"Show me how much by coming all over my hand."

I adjust myself so that my thumb can rub her clit while I finger her silly. At the same time, my other hand cups her chin, and I pull her head back, so I can kiss her mouth. She whimpers, and her hips press back against my cock. It's hard and straining against my jeans, but I don't care. I can wait to fuck her. What I can't do is wait to make her come. I need her release like I need to breathe.

With my thumb held against her swollen clit, I push a

third finger through her slickness to rub against her walls. When I find her ridge and push faster and deeper, I cover her mouth again. "That's it, baby, squeeze my fingers. Show me what you'll do to my cock later." She opens her mouth behind my hand, and I reward her with two fingers. She runs her tongue around them, sucking, while her pussy quivers around the three I'm using to fuck her. "Yes, I feel how close you are. Let me have it. Let it go." And she does. Her walls squeeze my fingers at the same time her fingertips turn white from how tightly she's gripping the countertop.

I pull my hand from her pants and wrap my arms around her, holding her up as she goes slack from the force of her release. She grabs my hand and pulls it up to her mouth, ready to lick my fingers clean.

"I earned a taste of that release, Mistress."

"You can let me have one," she says and sucks my middle finger all the way into her mouth, running her tongue around it to lick up every stop.

My cock jumps in my pants, ready to take its turn. She must feel it against her ass because she reaches back, her warm hand cupping it through the denim. Turning her head to look up at me with imploring eyes, Clarissa releases my finger. I pull my hand to my own mouth, licking up the other two that had been inside her. Her eyes stay locked on my mouth, pupils dilated and hungry.

"I have to go back to work," I say, kissing her cheek.

"Are you serious right now?" she asks, her voice lilting up as I extricate my bulge from her hand and step away slowly, making sure her legs are steady.

"We don't want to wake the children, and if I fuck you right now, we will wake the entire town." I'm only slightly exaggerating, but it doesn't stop her from glaring at me in disbelief. "I'll let you punish me later," I promise on my way out the tent. She mumbles something, but I can't hear her. I smile with the knowledge that she will make me pay for this later tonight.

Back at the truck, Peter's surrounded by pines laying on the ground while he pets the mangiest dog I've ever seen. Lucky looked a hot mess when I saved him from the mountainside, but that was nothing compared to worn out look of this pup.

"Made a new friend, I see."

Peter looks up at me and chuckles. "Yep, a couple of them." He tilts his chin toward a group standing across the makeshift road. There are two women and one older guy. One of the women, a caramel-skinned beauty, stares in this direction, her gaze locked on my friend. I turn back to him, and he just smirks.

"I was gonna ask if they wanted to buy a tree, but the look on her face says she'd rather climb you like a tree."

He smiles ear-to-ear, and I laugh. "Speaking of tree-climbing, how's Clarissa and my little niece?"

"Marissa and Lucky were both asleep when I found them all."

This statement only makes his smile grow until all his teeth are showing. "Well, that would explain why it took you so long to come back."

I just shake my head and observe how his gaze goes back and forth between me and the woman watching us. I tip my head toward her. "Why don't you go get lost for a little bit?" When he doesn't look like he's going to move, I add, "I'll get this mess cleaned up," with a sweeping gesture at the trees on the ground as added encouragement.

"You sure?"

"Man, get out of here."

He stands and walks off toward the trio, the dog following in his wake. The woman smiles up at him when he extends a hand, and the other two walk off hand-in-hand. Maybe I was wrong to complain about how late we arrived. It seems we had perfect timing.

At that thought, I start picking up the trees and leaning them against the truck, tying them to the sides of the trailer individually. We had already dropped off the ones we brought for the lumberjack wood-chopping competition. These trees are to sell with a goal to head back to the farm with an empty trailer. From the way Clarissa whined when I left, and the way this girl is looking at Peter, trees won't be the only wood being pushed this week.

Leya Layne

Leya Layne's love of a Happily Ever After started with Disney. Then she found romance novels in her early teens thanks to a bag of Harlequin novels hidden under her grandmother's dresser. She got her HEA fix for the rest of her teen years thanks to a well-worn library card. Though she is currently publishing contemporary romances that have been described as Hot Hallmark, don't be surprised to see her delve into historical or paranormal in the future. The possibilities are endless, but the one thing she'll promise is that they'll all be spicy!

Follow Leya all over social media:
https://linktr.ee/LeyaLayneAuthor

See her website for forthcoming releases and trigger/content warnings:
https://bisabelwrites.com/leyas-content-is-for-18-only/

Coming Soon

May 2025: Heating Up in Cole County: A Cozy Romance
Anthology

Fall 2025: Yet unnamed spooky novella